O

BABY ON BOARD

miniseries has grown!

Now you can share in even more tears and
triumphs as Harlequin Romance®
brings you a month full of

Pregnancy & Proposals, Miracles & Marriage!

Don't miss:

Adopted: Family in a Million
by Barbara McMahon

Hired: Nanny Bride
by Cara Colter

Italian Tycoon, Secret Son
by Lucy Gordon

Blind-Date Baby
by Fiona Harper

The Billionaire's Baby
by Nicola Marsh

Doorstep Daddy
by Shirley Jump

Dear Reader,

You are the reason Harlequin is celebrating sixty years of books that delight women all over the world. I'm happy to say I'm also an avid reader of Harlequin Romance® novels and have loved the books for more than half the time they've been published. As times change, the wonderful stories Harlequin Romance® brings also change to reflect current lifestyles. Though I loved the earlier books, and still reread a few on occasion, I enjoy today's books even more. The emotions touch me, the characters stay with me long after I read the last page and the happy feelings I get after the stories end boost my mood for a long time.

I'm delighted to be a part of Harlequin Romance®. I hope you enjoy *Adopted: Family in a Million* as much as I enjoyed writing it. Sometimes dreams are all we have and when they come true, it's a wondrous thing—even when the dreams change as our lives change.

Happy sixtieth, Harlequin!

Come celebrate the anniversary with us by being swept away into the wonderful world of our stories.

With love,

Barbara

BARBARA McMAHON

Adopted: Family in a Million

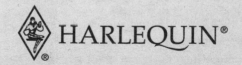

HARLEQUIN®

TORONTO • NEW YORK • LONDON
AMSTERDAM • PARIS • SYDNEY • HAMBURG
STOCKHOLM • ATHENS • TOKYO • MILAN • MADRID
PRAGUE • WARSAW • BUDAPEST • AUCKLAND

To my dear friend Carolyn Samuels.
Here's to fun in the sun
and happy memories of days gone by.

Recycling programs
for this product may
not exist in your area.

ISBN-13: 978-0-373-18439-2
ISBN-10:   0-373-18439-5

ADOPTED: FAMILY IN A MILLION

First North American Publication 2009.

Copyright © 2009 by Barbara McMahon.

www.eHarlequin.com

Printed in U.S.A.

Barbara McMahon was born and raised in the southern U.S.A., but settled in California after spending a year flying around the world for an international airline. After settling down to raise a family and work for a computer firm, she began writing when her children started school. Now, feeling fortunate in being able to realize a long-held dream of quitting her "day job" and writing full-time, she and her husband have moved to the Sierra Nevada of California, where she finds her desire to write is stronger than ever. With the beauty of the mountains visible from her windows, and the pace of life slower than that of the hectic San Francisco Bay Area, where they previously resided, she finds more time than ever to think up stories and characters and share them with others through writing. Barbara loves to hear from readers. You can reach her at P.O. Box 977, Pioneer, CA 95666-0977, U.S.A. Readers can also contact Barbara at her Web site, www.barbaramcmahon.com.

**Don't miss Barbara McMahon's
next Harlequin Romance® novel,**
Greek Boss, Dream Proposal
August 2009

PROLOGUE

November

"I HAVE a son." Zack said the words aloud. The reality wasn't there. The pain was. He tried to focus on the revelation in the letter and ignore the injuries that had landed him in the hospital with months of healing and physical therapy ahead before he was fit again. Shifting slightly, he reread the letter.

The letter was dated three months ago. Why had it taken so long to reach him? Being on a remote building site in the middle of a Middle Eastern desert probably had a lot to do with it.

Did it matter? What if it had arrived shortly after it had been posted, he would have still been in shock. Would it have changed anything? Would he have been on the phone asking questions instead of being in the vicinity of that land mine?

"I have a son and his name is Daniel," he repeated softly.

"Did you say something?" A nurse poked her

head into the room. "Everything okay? Need more painkiller?"

"I'm okay," he said, impatient with the interruption. He wanted to read the letter again. Try to understand.

He couldn't take it in. Alesia Blair had been his steady girlfriend the last time he had been Stateside on leave. They'd had a great few months together, until he had accepted another overseas assignment. There had been no great love between them, but he had enjoyed taking her places where others had admired her beauty. To think of her as dead was hard. She'd relished life.

But she'd never contacted him after he had left. Not even to tell him about their son.

He was grateful to her sister, Brittany, however, for letting him know, however delinquent the notice. She explained she had been against her sister's decision to keep quiet about the baby. A child should know his father. She'd wrestled with the situation after Alesia's death and finally decided to write to him, telling him what she knew. He'd railed against fate for Alesia's silence. How could she not have told him five years ago she was carrying his child?

At least he had the opportunity and means to locate the boy, his only living relative. That thought was amazing. He'd accepted years ago that he'd probably spend his life alone. He had friends, but no one close. His formative years had been in a series of foster homes. Moving from place to place had taught him not to form attachments. Nothing lasted beyond the next move. His job did nothing to change that as an adult. He was a nomad, no home, no family.

Zack had no idea when he had left the United States almost five years ago that Alesia had been pregnant. They had used precautions. She had never contacted him. At first he thought she might. But his job assignment had been for two years. Alesia had been a fun-loving, party girl. Two years waiting for a man was not her style. Yet the pregnancy would have changed all that.

She should have told him. Why hadn't she?

Her sister's letter also informed him of Alesia's death. For that he was truly sorry. She had been pretty and vivacious and fun. Which was probably the reason she'd given their son up for adoption. A baby would have definitely cramped her style.

But I could have taken him. The thought came out of nowhere. Zack didn't know the first thing about children. He was thirty-four years old and had never seriously thought about getting married or having a family.

His job was not exactly conducive to a happy family—gone two years at a time to inhospitable locales where they fought to bring modern roads and bridges and dams to countries that had progressed little from the beginning of time.

Lying back on the pillows, he tried to imagine his son. The boy would be four now. Zack couldn't remember back to when he had been four. He had already been placed in his first foster home by that age. There had been other children there, but his memories were hazy. What was a four-year-old like?

That led to wondering what the family who had adopted his son was like. Did they think his father had abandoned him? Did they know Zack had not even known of his son's existence until he'd received this letter a few hours ago?

He had an overwhelming urge to find his son. See him. Make sure he was happy and well cared for. Even in the foster care system, bad things happened to children. Did adopted families have regular visits from Social Services to make sure the child was being properly looked after? Was Daniel happy and secure in the family that was raising him?

Zack was scheduled to be sent back to the States next week—if he continued to improve. The surgeries had drained him of all energy. He was fighting to recover. But it would be several months before he could return to work. Just maybe he'd have time to find his son to make sure he was all right. To see what he and Alesia had produced.

Did Daniel have dark hair like his, or was it lighter like Alesia's blond hair? Was he fearful or brave? Adoptions were usually confidential. Did he really have any hope in the world of finding the child he'd fathered?

He picked up the paper and pen the nurse had provided. The least he could do was thank Brittany for letting him know. It had been the right thing to do. And just maybe, it had given him even more reason for getting fit again as soon as possible. He had a son to find.

April

"Here's the final report." Ben Abercrombie slid the folder across the desk. "I know it took longer than originally anticipated, but you know adoption records are hard to access. Here's what I found out. Your son was adopted by T. J. and Susan Johnson of New York City. I've located Mrs. Johnson, the husband has since died. Killed by a drunk driver two years ago."

Zack Morgan reached out for the folder and flipped it open. The first thing he saw was a picture of a small child. It was not a close up, but he could tell the boy had dark hair. He looked so little. Was he small for his age? Zack had no idea how big four-year-olds should be.

Ben frowned as he glanced at the paperwork. "So how did you want this handled? Just show up one day and ask to meet your son?"

Zack shook his head. "Despite what you may think, I have some feelings for the child and the situation. The last thing I would do is give any reason to rock his security." He thought briefly of the different families he'd lived with. He never knew how long he'd stay. He couldn't imagine deliberately causing that kind of panic and uncertainty to anyone, much less a little boy.

"I just want to know he's okay. That he's loved and the family life he has is good."

The detective leaned back in his chair, steepling his hands. "Mother appears to be doing the best she can. It was a comedown from the lifestyle they enjoyed when the husband was alive. He was an attorney and made a good income. Since his death, they've moved to a less affluent neighborhood. She's gone back to work. Still, from what I could see, the mother takes good care of the child and he seems happy enough. Quiet, not as boisterous as other little kids I've seen. But, hey, everyone has a different personality."

"But he's got a good mother, right?" Zack couldn't remember his own mother. The best foster mom had been Allie Zumwalt. He hoped Daniel had a mother as sweet as Allie.

Ben nodded. "Doing the best she can."

"What do you mean by that?" Zack asked quickly.

"She has to work, leaves the child with an older woman in their building. The apartment building is old, a bit run-down. The neighborhood's not the best place to be after dark."

"Should they move?"

"Takes money to live where they did before. New York's not a cheap city."

The one thing Zack had was money. He spent little, had amassed a small fortune working overseas with the extra hardship pay. Judicial investments had the money growing steadily. The detective had delivered, and the cost had been nothing Zack wouldn't have paid three times over or more to find out about his son.

He looked at the photograph again. Would he recognize the child if he tripped over him in a crowd somewhere? Shouldn't there be some kind of tie between biological parents and children? Some sort of instant connection? To Zack, there was nothing but wonder that he could have fathered this little boy.

Railing silently against Alesia once again, he closed the folder and stood. "Thank you," he said, offering his hand.

"I'll be here if you want anything else," the detective said.

Zack carried the folder out with him. He was staying in a small hotel near Central Park while he finished recuperating. He could walk without the limp as long as he didn't overdo it. His shoulder was still stiff. Maybe he needed to get back to work to loosen those muscles. But he was on medical leave and still doing his physical therapy routine each day.

When he reached his room, he settled down to read every word in the report the detective had compiled. Even if he never got to meet him, Zack knew he'd left a legacy to the future. Thinking about it, he could do more. On Monday, he'd make an appointment with an attorney to leave his estate to his son. They may never meet, but someday Daniel would know his father had cared about him.

CHAPTER ONE

SUSAN JOHNSON was frantic. She could scarcely think as she rushed down the crowded New York sidewalk, dodging pedestrians, searching for her son. How could one small boy disappear so quickly. Why wasn't someone looking for his mother? When she found him, she'd never let him out of her sight again!

Of course that was impossible, but she was so scared she couldn't think straight. Where was Danny?

"Please, God, let me find my baby," she prayed as she searched the crowded sidewalk in front of her.

"Do you think he'd try to cross the street alone?" the teacher's aide next to her asked, already puffing slightly from the fast pace Susan set.

"No. I don't know. If he thought he saw his father across the street he might, though I'm always careful to make sure we stop and look both ways even when the light is green. But he's only four." And always after tall dark haired men thinking they were his daddy. Ever since Tom had died, Danny had been searching. Children his age didn't understand death, she'd been told.

How could the preschool have let him get away? The play yard was fenced and the front gate should have either been latched so a little child couldn't open it, or monitored by an adult. Had the teacher turned her back? For how long? Where was Danny?

Were they going in the wrong direction? Had he turned right when exiting the preschool? Or left? She'd opted for left because it was in the direction of their apartment. Familiar territory to a little boy. But what if he'd gone the other way? If he'd darted out to follow some stranger, he wouldn't have cared for direction—only his goal to find his father. She could be increasing the distance between them, not closing it. Panic closed her throat. Fear seized her heart. Her precious son was out on the streets of New York and could get into who knew what kind of trouble.

Susan stopped and looked ahead, then behind her. Indecision. Seconds were ticking by. Where was her child? Fear increased. New York was a dangerous city. And her son was adorable. What if someone snatched him up? What if she never saw him again?

She moaned softly at the thought.

Her child was missing. Was there anything worse for a parent to face?

"What?" the aide asked.

"I'm thinking he could have gone the other way.

Tell me again how long ago it was until you noticed he was missing?" Susan had been given all that information when she had arrived at the preschool. But she'd scarcely listened, dashing out to try to find her son.

"Less than five minutes before you showed up. Mrs. Savalack was busy with the little boy who had a bloody nose. She didn't know Danny would leave before you arrived. She went the other direction as soon as one of the other teachers came to watch her children. She'll find him if he went that way."

"Maybe," Susan said, her eyes searching. She didn't see a child anywhere.

Glancing around, she noticed a man walking slowly along the street. He looked out of place in the midday crowd—ambling along when everyone else was walking briskly, with places to go. Tall, with dark hair and a deep tan, he looked competent and reliable. His casual attire blended in with the men and women on the sidewalk at the lunch hour, but were of higher quality than the cheaper clothing more common in this neighborhood. What a stupid thing to notice, she thought as she approached him.

"Excuse me. Have you seen a little boy? He's four and should not be out on his own. We don't know if he came this way, but we need to find him!"

He shook his head. "I haven't seen any kids. Wouldn't they be in school at this time of day?"

"He's in a preschool and wandered away." Susan

bit her lip, her heart pounded, fear increasing with every heartbeat. "Maybe I'm going the wrong way."

"Which way is that?" he asked, glancing at the aide and then scanning the sidewalk behind him.

"No one saw him leave, so we didn't know if he came this way or went the other way. The preschool is back there." She pointed to a small building at the end of the block. "I just hope he didn't try to cross the street." The traffic was lighter than midtown, but still heavy. A small boy might be overlooked by a motorist in a hurry—until it was too late.

"Someone would have stopped a small boy from dashing into danger," the man said. He glanced at the aide. "Is someone looking in the other direction?"

"Yes, the teacher." She glanced back up the street. "I don't see her, so I guess she hasn't found Danny."

"Danny?" the man asked, his voice odd.

Susan looked at him, her eyes holding appeal. "My son, Danny. He's missing. I've got to find him. Oh Lord, I can't lose him, too!"

"I'll help look. Name's Zack Morgan. Where did you lose him?"

"I didn't lose him. He left his preschool without an adult. I can't believe he's run off like this. New York is so dangerous for a little child if someone isn't right there with him every minute."

"I'm sure he'll be fine, Mrs. Johnson," the aide said, her worried expression belying her words.

"We'll find him," Zack said.

"Unless someone's taken him," Susan said, voicing her worst fear. What if someone had kidnapped her son? She swayed with horror at the thought. Zack reached out and took her arm gently, seeming to give her strength.

"No one's taken him in this direction. I've been on this street for several blocks. No little boy. And I'm sure no one would let him cross the street by himself, so let's try the other direction." His reasonable tone calmed her.

"Okay." For a split second she felt as if the burden had lifted slightly and been placed on the broad shoulders of the stranger who held her arm.

She swallowed and turned, wanting to race the wind to find her son. He was so precious to her. He could not have been taken. He was just searching for Tom.

Less than five minutes later they saw Mrs. Savalack heading toward them, Danny's hand firmly held in hers.

Susan burst into tears and raced to her son. "Danny, you scared me to death." She swooped him up in her arms, hugging him tightly, her heart still pounding. "Don't ever run off like that again."

He struggled a bit with Susan's tight hold, and she set him on his feet, taking his hand firmly in hers. "You know you are not to leave the school until I get there."

"I thought I saw Daddy." He looked sad. "But it wasn't him."

Susan reached out and brought Danny's face round to face hers. "Your daddy died. He's gone to heaven. You will not find him on this earth. Honey, he loved you, but he's gone."

"No! I want my daddy!" Danny stuck his lower lip out and glared at his mother.

The stranger stooped down until he was Danny's level.

"Hi," he said.

Danny looked at him warily, pout still in evidence.

"You should mind your mother," Zack said gently. "She was scared you'd get hurt or lost." He reached out and brushed Danny's dark hair off his forehead.

"I thought I saw my daddy," Danny repeated.

Susan wiped the tears from her cheeks and tried to smile at Zack. "He's got this fixation in his head that my husband is just gone out. Every time he sees a man who looks the slightest bit like Tom, he's running after him. He hasn't done this in a long while and I'd hoped he'd stopped by now. Thanks for your help. I'm Susan Johnson. This is my son, Danny. I appreciate your concern."

Zack rose and nodded. "You two take care now."

He turned and walked away, when every cell in his body screamed to stay. He'd actually touched his son. Met his adopted mother. Been scared for a few moments that Susan Johnson's fear would turn into reality.

It had been a quirky idea to wander by the pre-school the detective had listed in his report. Zack had had no idea whether the playground could be seen from the street. Or if he'd recognize his son among a few dozen playing children. Fate had stepped in and he had actually spoken to his son.

He had thought that seeing Daniel from a distance would suffice. Now that he'd actually met him, he wanted to know even more about him. He was adorable. His eyes were brown and his hair a darker brown. He seemed small, but so did the other children Zack glimpsed in the playground. Daniel obviously missed his father. The report said Tom Johnson had died two years ago, which meant Danny had been grieving for two years. A long time for a child. Wasn't he happy with his mother?

Wanting to think about the encounter, Zack walked a few more blocks until he found a coffee house. Ordering a hot drink, he sat at a table near the window and gazed outside, his thoughts back with the boy he'd just met. And his mother.

There had been no photo of Susan in the report. She looked younger than he expected. And tired. She was thin like Alesia had been. But where Alesia had always worn trendy, stylish clothing, Susan's looked plain and serviceable. Her hair had been pulled back and she wore a minimum of makeup. The appeal in her eyes when she asked if he'd seen her son had touched him. He could tell she loved the boy.

For some reason, Zack felt a need to do something for her as well. It couldn't be easy raising a child alone. She had no relatives close by. According to the detective, her parents lived in Florida. Her mother worked in a travel agency and her father was in frail health. The warmer climate was a necessity for his well-being in winter months.

Her dead husband had been the only child of an older couple. His mother had moved west to be with her sister when her husband had died before Tom and Susan were married. She now resided in an assisted care home in California.

There had been little insurance money; the man had been younger than Zack was now when he had died. They must have thought they had their entire future together. Neither had known two years after adopting Danny that Tom Johnson would be dead.

Would they still have gone through with the adoption?

Zack felt funny knowing so much about Susan Johnson and her family history. She didn't know him at all except as a stranger stopping to help for a few minutes. Yet he wanted to know about her, to assure himself his son was getting the best of everything. And with the dearth of money in her life, was that possible?

Maybe he could set up a blind trust to make sure they had enough money. Would Susan accept? The character sketch the detective had done indicated she probably would not. She seemed big on independence. She hadn't applied for any aid. She'd quickly moved from the apartment she and her husband shared in Manhattan to one more affordable in Brooklyn. Even returned to work when she'd obviously planned to stay home with Danny if the first two years of his life were any indication.

He sipped his coffee and wondered what he could do. Maybe the best thing would be to leave mother and son alone. Danny looked healthy. His clothes had been neat and clean. He obviously missed his father, but he was well cared for.

For a moment Zack wondered what it would be like to be a father to a child. He'd have to change his job, quit the nomadic life he'd enjoyed the last decade and put down roots. Get a job that would allow him to be home evenings, attend school events.

Would he grow bored? Long for faraway lands?

Slowly Zack smiled. Danny was a cute kid. His dark hair probably came from him. And his brown eyes. Did he look at all like Alesia? With soft baby cheeks, it was hard to tell. He wished he had some baby pictures of himself. Maybe he could see a resemblance to himself at that age.

He finished his coffee and rose. He'd walk by their apartment and then return to his hotel. It would be enough to know where they lived. Then he had to think about what he wanted to do for the rest of his medical leave. Walking had been strongly recommended, as had light exercise in addition to the P.T. he was doing. He had an entire schedule for the next couple of months tacked to the mirror in the bathroom. By then he should be ready to return to the Middle East and work.

He needed to decide on what to do about the future, but there was no rush. He had time.

Danny jumped up and down, his face shining with excitement. "Let's go, Mommy. Let's go!"

"In a minute, sweetie. I need to get some bottled water and a snack for us. You know you always get hungry at the park." Susan smiled at her son as she headed to the kitchen to gather what she needed. Yesterday's scare had faded to the background, but hadn't totally disappeared. She sometimes didn't know if she was going to make it as a single mother. Danny was a handful. Somehow she had to get him over chasing after strangers thinking they were Tom.

Yesterday's trauma had been a strain but everything was fine—for now. Danny loved going to the park. Actually he loved going anywhere—to the store, preschool, visiting Mrs. Jordan, her neighbor who watched Danny when Susan had to work.

Susan put some dried fruit and two water bottles in the small backpack, checked to make sure the sunscreen was there and the wet-wipes. Picking up her dark glasses, she was ready. This spring had proved balmy and warm for New York City. She took advantage of the nearby park every chance she got. The grassy area gave plenty of running room for Danny and the playground section provided slides and swings and other equipment that he loved. It was a great way for him to burn off some of that energy he had.

Their apartment was tiny. It was all she could afford with her salary and the expense of preschool and Edith's pay. The neighborhood wasn't the best, but it was the best she could afford and be close enough to work that she didn't spend hours commuting. She'd rather spend the time with Danny.

Passing through the crowded living room she glanced at Tom's picture out of habit. She still missed him with an ache that never seemed to go away despite the two years that had passed since his death. They'd taken Danny for walks together before he died, but Danny had been in the stroller then. Wouldn't Tom have loved watching Danny at the park playing with the other children—running around, yelling in sheer joy?

"Okay, I'm ready." She smiled at her son, her heart swelling with love. He was such a darling boy. She wished Tom had lived to see Danny grow up. He'd been as excited as she when Danny had come into their lives. They'd made such plans for the future—family vacations, maybe buying a house one day with a yard so Danny could have a dog. Tom had wanted him to attend NYU. Sighing softly for what was not to be, she helped her son put his jacket on. It was up to her to make sure Tom's dreams came true.

"Yay!" Danny ran to the front door and waited impatiently while his mother unlocked it and opened it. He was off like a shot to the elevator. "I can push the button," Danny said proudly and pressed the down arrow.

Susan locked her door and hurried to follow her son. She wouldn't put it past him to jump into the elevator without her in his excitement to get to the park.

Danny raced out of the elevator when it reached the lobby.

"Danny, wait!" She hurried after him and took his hand before he reached the large glass door that led outside.

Danny did not move slowly. She laughed as they raced the light at the corner. In only moments they reached the grassy expanse. Releasing Danny's hand, she followed as he headed directly to the playground area. Several children she recognized were already running around, swinging, sliding down the slides and having a great time. Danny joined in with no hesitation.

Susan glanced around at the benches, looking for an empty seat. She spotted the man she'd met briefly yesterday, Zack Morgan. Did he live in the neighborhood? She didn't remember seeing him before. And he was someone she would have remembered. Slowly she walked over. He looked up when she drew near and nodded in greeting.

"Good morning," he said.

His voice was amazing, deep and husky. She remembered how tall he was. Even sitting, he gave the impression of strength and size. His hair was almost black. A dark tan gave him a healthy look, while faint lines around his eyes proved he squinted in bright sunshine. Spring had been nice, but not that nice. Was he a skier? That would explain the tan so early in the season. He was broad in the shoulders, muscular without appearing to be a bodybuilder. He looked totally out of place in the park. She glanced back at Danny. Seeing the man had her thinking of wide-open spaces and endless vistas. A man used to doing, not sitting. Why was he in the park today? Did he live nearby? Had he been a regular she'd overlooked before meeting him?

For an instant she had the insane urge to make sure her hair was tidy and she still wore lipstick.

She looked back and smiled politely. After a second's hesitation, she sat beside him.

"I'm sorry I didn't thank you properly yesterday," she said.

"I didn't find your child. The teacher did."

"Just being willing to help was a good thing. I

appreciate it. And the fact that you looked. Many people would have been too busy."

"I'm glad he was safe," Zack said, glancing over at the children. The folded newspaper at his side indicated he'd been there for some time. Did he have a child playing with the others?

"I'm Susan Johnson." She reached out to shake his hand. His palm was hard, callused. His grip was firm without being too hard. The tingling sensation that ran up her arm surprised her and she pulled back quickly, more aware of the man than she ought to have been.

"We met yesterday. You were a bit flustered, though. No lasting aftereffects after your scare?"

"Just a constant worry of that child of mine making me gray way before my time," she replied, sitting back and relaxing, her gaze on Danny. She was not taking the chance he'd run after some other man today.

After a few moments of silence, she glanced at Zack and was surprised to find him watching the children play. Somehow he didn't seem like a man who spent a lot of time with children.

He noted her look and returned her gaze. "I haven't seen kids play like this in a long time. I've been on assignment overseas for the last five years."

"Are you in the military?" she asked, curious.

"No, construction. We've been building bridges and dams and housing projects in the Middle East. When I had leave, I toured Europe. I'm on leave right now—enforced unfortunately. Got too close to a land mine."

"Oh my gosh," she said. "I'm sorry. Are you all right?"

"Things will work out. I'm back on my feet and everything is functioning. But it'll take a little while until I'm one hundred percent again. I've been gone overseas so long, I feel like a stranger in my own country."

"You'll get used to things quickly, I bet. Are you from New York?"

"No. Originally from Chicago. But I haven't lived there in fifteen years. I'm thinking of subletting an apartment close to the hospital where I'm getting physical therapy until I decide where to settle."

"You picked a great place to recuperate. I love New York. I'm from here originally and can't imagine living anywhere else."

"Hard place to raise a kid, though, isn't it? Don't you wish for a backyard where he could play safely by himself? Maybe get a dog? A safer neighborhood?" Zack asked.

Susan took a breath, startled that he captured the ideal Tom had often voiced. Was it a universal male thing? Her defenses rose when he mentioned a safer neighborhood. It was something she thought about a lot. The few blocks surrounding their apartment were not the best in the city, but it was the best she could afford. It wasn't too much of a problem while Danny was still little. She worried about when he got older. What if he fell in with the wrong crowd. Even a gang. She would like a better home, but her talents were limited and she earned more where she was than a teacher would. Which was the only other thing she had trained for. But she wasn't sharing that with a stranger, no matter how much he interested her.

"He's too young to take proper care of a dog. Maybe when he's older. Pets are allowed in our building, you know." There would be no house with a yard for them.

"Oh," Zack said.

"The preschool he goes to two mornings a week is close, as is shopping. And I don't have the upkeep of a yard."

"Do you work nearby?" he asked.

"At the UN. I'm a translator. German."

And lucky to get such a well-paying job after her husband's death. They'd planned on her staying home with the baby, not having a day care provider be with their child all day. Unfortunately things didn't turn out that way.

"And your husband?"

She took a deep breath. The shock of loss still startled her. "He died a couple of years ago. He was an attorney." Susan sought Danny. He laughed as he slid down the slide, chased by two friends. She smiled at his happiness. So often he lapsed into sulks with his father gone. He and Tom had enjoyed a special bond by the time Danny turned two.

"Sorry to hear about your loss. Cute kid you have."

"I'm so grateful for Danny. He kept me going when Tom died."

Susan watched her son. She didn't want him to forget Tom, so she had photographs all around the apartment. She told him stories about Tom as a boy. And about how they had met and got married. She wanted Tom to be a part of his life even though Danny's memories would fade over time. She wondered even now if he had any real memories, or just the stories she told about his daddy, and the pictures he saw every day.

Sometimes Susan couldn't remember a detail or two. She'd panic and search in her mind. She never wanted to forget anything about the man she'd loved so much.

"Do you have a child here?" Susan asked, looking at all the children. There had to be twenty, of all ages from toddlers with their mothers nearby to children aged seven or eight.

"No. I just wanted a place to sit in the sun and read the paper. It was only after I was here a while that children started arriving. The playground is quite a draw, isn't it?"

"Closest playground in this area. With all the apartments around here, you know there're lots of kids," she explained. "We come as often as we can.

It's a great way for Danny to play with friends and get fresh air and sunshine. Probably not so appealing to people who want to also enjoy the fresh air but not have the noise."

Zack shrugged. "It suits me. I like to watch them. I know very little about children. I live in a world of men in a harsh environment. No grass where I've been the last eighteen months. This is like an oasis."

"Where have you been?"

"In a small country in the Arabian desert. We were building a dam across a river. The lake behind it will give irrigation to hundreds of acres for agricultural purposes."

"Did someone protest?"

"No." He looked puzzled.

"You said you are recovering from a land mine explosion," Susan said.

"Oh, that. I was temporarily assigned to another site our company is handling, closer to the war zone. That's where the mine was."

"Anyone else hurt?"

He shook his head. "One man killed, but no one else injured."

"That's awful."

"It's amazing how life can change in an instant," he said. "Or end as quickly."

She nodded. "That's what happened to me. One minute my husband was alive and on his way home from work, the next dead when a drunk driver ran a red light and killed him. No warning. No time for goodbyes."

He glanced at her but she watched Danny. The aching grief was never far away. "That must have been tough. Especially with a child."

She nodded. "But we're getting by," she said—to convince Zack or herself?

Zack had taken a chance that Susan Johnson would bring Danny to the park this morning. The weather forecast had been for a warm day and he hoped she was in the habit of letting her son play outside. He'd read the entire newspaper and about given up when he'd seen them cross the street. Patience was not a virtue he considered he had. But it had paid off today.

And luck, as well, when she joined him on the bench. There were other empty spots she could have chosen. He was glad she sat beside him.

The more she spoke, the more he wanted to know about her. There was sadness in her eyes. She still grieved her husband. But when she looked at Danny, she seemed to light up inside.

How would it feel to have someone look at him that way? He hoped his mother had at least one time, but he would never know. He'd never met a woman who loved him. He wasn't sure it was possible. There had to be something wrong with someone who had been abandoned by his parents, shuffled around in foster care and unable to make a lasting commitment.

Zack frowned. That wasn't true. He had made a commitment to work and stuck by it despite the real hardships and uncomfortable—even danger-ous—living conditions.

But relationships were different.

He hadn't even warranted a note from Alesia telling him about his son.

He shifted slightly, trying to ease the ache in his back. He was stiffening up. He needed to walk again. But he hated to leave. He might never get another opportunity like this to speak with the woman who was now mother to his child.

There was so much to find out.

"Are you staying nearby?" Susan asked.

He nodded. "In a small hotel." Nearby was relative. The hotel was certainly closer than his work site. It required a subway ride and a walk of several blocks, but he wasn't going to tell her that if he didn't need to.

"I wish I knew of someone subletting an apart-ment or something," she said. "It has to be costly to stay in a hotel, no matter how modest."

Zack decided not to tell her the company was picking up the expenses. All medical costs as well. Then what she said registered. She would suggest a place for him to sublet? Close enough he might see Susan and Danny again? He hadn't thought about getting to know them. He'd only wanted to make sure his son was healthy and happy.

He had at least two more months, maybe longer, before the doctor would certify him for work. He could spend some of it here—with the woman beside him and his son.

"I appreciate the thought," he said.

She frowned. "I'll ask around. There has to be something, though sublets get snapped up fast. Housing is so expensive here."

"Why not move to a more affordable place?"

"This is the closest apartment to the UN I could afford. I don't want to spend any more time away from Danny than I have to, which moving out farther would entail."

He hadn't thought about that. There was a lot more involved to family life than he'd originally considered. Maybe he should look for a sublet closer to the UN, in a nicer neighborhood, and then give it to Susan when he left.

"I guess you won't be here long enough for a sublet," she mused.

"Another two or three months. If someone was traveling or something, I could house-sit. But not for longer than that."

"I'll let you know if I hear anything," she said. "How can I reach you?"

Zack started to say just look for me here every day, but thought better of it. He reached into his pocket for his wallet, withdrawing one of his business cards. He stared at it. He couldn't remember the phone number of the hotel and if he told her the name she'd know it wasn't that close.

He looked at her. "I don't remember the hotel number. Tell you what, I'll get a cell phone later today and if you're here tomorrow, give that number to you." He held out his card to her. "In the meantime, this is information about the company I work for. In emergencies, they can always contact employees. They know where we are."

"Okay." She smiled and then took the card. The company was a well-known construction firm that built large-scale buildings, dams and roads world-wide.

For a moment Susan wanted to give her number to this stranger. She'd run into him briefly yesterday and then again today. She didn't know him from Adam, but he had helped her yesterday. He didn't know where she lived, so couldn't be following her. If he were staying around here, this park was a nice place to sit in the sunshine.

He interested her in a way a man hadn't in a long time.

She felt suddenly alive around him.

Blinking, she looked away. For some reason he seemed more confident and secure than the men she usually saw on a daily basis—without being over-bearing or arrogant.

She checked on Danny again and then looked around at the other benches occupied with parents and others visiting the park. She always kept watch to make sure Danny was safe. Today she'd forgotten to pay attention to Danny every second. He was fine, but it was unlike her to forget him even for a second.

Being with Zack stirred her senses and made her more curious than warranted. And had her offering to help where no help was asked for. Maybe he liked living in a hotel. Why had she opened her mouth and made such an impulsive offer? It was unlike her. Or at least the her she'd been the last couple of years.

Susan waved to Danny when he yelled to her. He ran over, eyeing Zack suspiciously.

"Come and have a drink of water. You've been running around so much," she said, drawing a bottle of water from her tote.

"Who is that?" Danny asked, staring at Zack.

"The man who helped me look for you yesterday, remember? Zack Morgan," Susan said.

Danny drank his water and then smiled. "Hi," he said.

"Hi yourself," Zack replied. He studied the child for a moment then smiled. "You like the slides I can tell."

"Yes. I can climb up all by myself and then go down. Watch." Danny thrust the water back at Susan and ran back to the slide, waiting his turn to mount the stairs and slide down. He looked at Zack with pride.

Zack made a thumbs-up sign.

"He's so proud of his accomplishments," Susan

said. "I keep hoping he'll adjust to his father's death. He keeps looking for Tom whenever we go out."

"Tough break for both of you," Zack said.

Susan nodded. "And scary if he runs off like yesterday."

Zack stretched slowly and then rose. "I have to get moving. I'm stiffening up," he said. He reached for the paper and looked at Susan. "Want this or shall I toss it?"

"I'll take it if you're finished with it. Are you okay?"

"I will be, just need to keep moving. Nice to talk to you."

"We'll come tomorrow, you can give me your phone number and I'll let you know if I hear of a sublet." She watched as he walked away. She could tell he was in pain. She hadn't noticed a limp yesterday, but he definitely was favoring his left leg as he slowly walked on the path through the park. Once he reached the sidewalk, it wasn't long before he was lost from view.

Susan studied his card. Zackary Morgan, engineer. He was as different from Tom as any man she knew. His hand had been callused and hard. He was tanned and rugged. He lived in foreign countries and did work only a very few could handle. Yet their paths had crossed and Susan was glad for it.

She may have been a tad pushy about offering to find him a place, but she wanted to do something for him. He'd offered her help yesterday. Now it was her turn.

Was that all? To repay his offer? She refused to dwell on why, but she hoped she had not seen the last of Zackary Morgan.

CHAPTER TWO

SUNDAY it rained. Susan was disappointed. There would be no going to the park that day. After breakfast, she stood at the window for a little while, watching the water trace down the pane. It was not a quick shower that would end soon. She had wanted to take Danny out.

And maybe run into Zack.

Sighing softly, she turned and went to gather the laundry. It was a chore she never relished. The dark basement that housed the two washing machines for their building gave her the creeps. She wished it could be painted and more light added. At least she didn't have to go to a public laundry and wait. So far no one had taken her clothes when she had left them in the apartment laundry.

It was early afternoon when the phone rang. Susan answered quickly. Danny was sleeping and she didn't want him to waken.

"Hi, darling," her mother greeted her.

"Hi, Mom."

"Your father's napping, so I thought I'd call." Her mother usually called once every week or so from Florida. Susan missed her parents and relished their chats on the phone.

"Danny's sleeping, too," Susan said, settling down on the sofa.

"How are things?" her mother asked.

"Okay. Danny scared me to death on Friday." Quickly Susan gave her mother a recap. "I don't know what to do with his chasing after men thinking they are Tom."

"He'll grow out of it sooner or later," her mom said.

"But in the meantime, I could die of fright if he disappears again. Or he could seriously get lost or abducted."

"What he needs is a father figure. That's what he's missing. I wished we lived closer. Your father loves the time he spends with Danny."

The image of Zack Morgan rose. She frowned. Why had he sprung to mind when her mother spoke of a father figure? He was the last person who would be interested in children. He said he hadn't been around them. His job would not be good for any kind of family life.

But she could fantasize. That he'd ask her out. That he'd like to spend time with Danny. The bubble burst. The only dates she'd had in the last two years had not ended well. She resigned herself to her single status—at least for another ten years or so.

"I worry about you two living in that neighborhood," her mother was saying.

"We've been through this, Mom. It's the best I can do."

"You could move down here. It's less expensive."

"And do what?"

"Teach."

"I love my job. It's exciting and keeps me up on all the world events."

"But you are so far away and we miss seeing Danny."

Susan refrained from reminding her mother they had moved away three years ago, not her. Florida offered a better climate for her father. She missed them, even more after Tom had died. But she did not want to move there herself. She'd miss New York too much. Besides, she was managing fine.

"I'll send more pictures," she offered.

"It's not the same. I'll call back later and talk with Danny," her mother said.

"He'd like that, Mom."

They chatted a few more minutes. Susan hung up and leaned back on the sofa. It was still raining. She might have chanced the park had it been warmer. Just to walk over in case Zack had walked there for exercise. She could tell he had been in pain yesterday sitting on the bench. She wished she knew more about his injuries and if he would completely recover. She hoped so. He looked too virile and active to be satisfied with a desk job when he could be out building mammoth structures.

The rainy weather continued until Friday and by Saturday morning, Susan was anxious to get to the park. She'd asked around about a place to sublet and a woman at work knew of one.

That was the only reason she wanted to see Zack, she told herself. To tell him about the apartment before it was taken.

Danny was delighted to be heading to the park after so many days inside. He had tried Edith Jordan's patience by Thursday and she'd been glad for preschool on Friday.

When they reached the park, Danny dashed to the playground. Susan looked at each bench. No sign of Zack.

Only when she felt the sweep of disappointment did she realize how much she had hoped to see him again.

She sat on the bench they'd shared last week and watched Danny play. The usual group of children were here. She waved at a couple of mothers she knew but didn't walk over to talk with them. Maybe Zack would still show up.

It was getting close to lunchtime. She hoped Danny wouldn't put up a fuss to return home. She had some chores to do and wanted to call one of her friends and discuss dinner one night next week. Laura had a son a year older than Danny. The two boys loved to play together.

She glanced around as a sixth sense kicked in. Zack was crossing the grass, a white bag held in one hand. His gaze was focused on her as he cut the distance swiftly. No sign of a limp today.

"Hi," he said when he was close.

"Hi." Susan felt fluttery inside. She had hoped to see him, but now that he was here, she felt positively shy. That was so not like her.

He lifted the bag a couple of inches. "I took a chance and brought coffee. If you don't want any, that's okay. I even brought some apple juice for Danny."

"I'd love a cup of coffee. I've only had one so far today and sitting here in the sun was making me sleepy."

He nodded and sat beside her. In seconds she was sipping the heavenly brew.

"I brought cream in case," he said, rummaging around in the bag.

"No, I like it black."

"Me, too." He lifted a bottle of apple juice and a straw, setting them on the bench between them.

Susan was touched he'd thought to bring something for Danny.

"Thank you." She caught Danny's attention and waved him over. He ran all the way.

"Hi," Zack said.

"Hi. Did you come to watch me play?" he asked.

Zack smiled and nodded. "I sure did."

"Zack brought you some apple juice," Susan said, opening the bottle and removing the wrapper from the straw.

"I love apple juice!" Danny exclaimed. He drank almost half the bottle and then stopped, gasping for breath.

"You don't need to drink it all in one go," his mother commented wryly. "What do you say?"

"Thank you for my apple juice," he said to Zack. Then he turned and ran back to the swings.

"Does he ever get tired?" Zack asked.

"Oh, yeah. After lunch he'll sleep for about two hours. Then be raring to go until bedtime. I'm glad you came today. I have a lead on a sublet, if you're still interested."

"I am. I spent the better part of this week looking."

Susan reached into the backpack and pulled out the note with the information about the small apartment not too far from a subway stop. She handed it to Zack. She wished it had been closer to this neighborhood. It would take some effort to come to the park from that place.

He read the information she'd jotted down then reached into his pocket and pulled out his wallet. He extracted another business card, then put her note in its place. Taking a pen, he wrote a phone number and handed her the card.

"I also bought a cell phone this week. Here's my number. Just in case."

"In case of what?" she asked, taking the card.

He shrugged. "You find another place available, or just want to talk."

She wondered if he was lonely. Though she couldn't imagine any woman would resist long if he showed some interest.

Including her.

"Thanks." She hesitated a moment. "I can give you our number if you like."

Zack nodded and in a moment had her number on the same paper as the sublet information.

"What did you do all week?" she asked.

"Worked on the physical therapy on my shoulder and hip. Hurts like crazy. They didn't tell me that when I started. Just some discomfort they said. Ha, I'd like to see them try it." He rotated his shoulder and grimaced. "Then I called about vacancies. Everything was taken by the time I called."

"You aren't trying to get back in shape in a week, are you?"

"Hey, no pain, no gain. Besides, I've been working on this since last November. "

"You need to follow instructions exactly for maximum recovery," she murmured.

"You a nurse?" He glanced at her. His dark eyes held amusement.

She grinned. It was fun to banter with him. "Better, I'm a mom. I know things. Didn't your mother tell you not to argue back?"

His look became pensive and he looked across the playground to where Danny and his friends were climbing the bars. "I don't remember my mother," he said.

"Oh." Susan was stricken. She couldn't have known he had lost his mother early. "I'm sorry," she said. She couldn't imagine her mother not being a part of her life, even though she lived in Florida.

He shrugged. "Things happen."

She longed to ask some questions, but didn't want to pry. If he wanted her to know more, he'd tell her.

Seeking a safe topic, she remembered the sublet. "My friend said the apartment will be sublet fully furnished. They want less than six months. They're taking a long tour of Europe, but not so long to tie up the place for a year. I thought it might work out."

"The way places get rented around here, I'll call this afternoon."

Susan sipped her coffee, feeling happier than she had in a long time. The day was beautiful, a cloudless blue sky, just enough breeze to keep the temperature from climbing uncomfortably high. She was watching her son have a great time. And sitting beside one of the most gorgeous men on the planet. She even caught a glimpse of some other mothers staring, and then talking among themselves. She resisted the urge to glance at Zack. Did he feel awkward being the only male around? No, wait, there were two fathers with their children playing Frisbee on the grass. But Zack wasn't with a child.

He took the last drink from his coffee and put the cup in the bag.

"I thought about seeing the sights, showing myself New York so to speak. Would you and your son like to go to the zoo with me tomorrow? I've seen nothing but sand and more sand in the last few years. It occurs to me that kind of outing would be more fun with a child along who would really be captivated by the animals."

Susan drew in a breath, surprised at the strong inclination to accept on the spot. She'd love to spend more time with him. Yet—she wasn't sure she was ready to date. She'd tried it twice and hated both outings. Was this a date? She didn't know the man, but they would be in a public place. How dangerous could going to the zoo be? Danny loved the zoo. They'd gone twice last summer.

"Let me check my calendar when I get home," she said, stalling. She wanted to think this through before making a decision. "It is fun to visit the exhibits with a little boy who's fascinated by everything. He's a bundle of energy and won't settle for a sedate pace."

"I checked—the zoo opens at nine, so I thought an early start to see as much as we can. I warn you, I may not have the stamina to last all day."

"Sounds like fun. I'll let you know. Thanks for inviting us to join you. Danny loves animals."

Zack nodded. He had asked. It was up to her. His gaze was drawn again to his son. The wonder was hard to accept. When Danny's laughter rang out, Zack wanted to scoop him up and hug him. He could watch this child for hours, fascinated to know he and Alesia had produced such a darling boy.

Anger simmered at his former lover for keeping this miracle from him. He would have dropped everything to return to the States if she'd only told him. Now he'd missed the opportunity to be a part of his life.

When Danny got in line for the large, curved slide, he was hidden from view for a few moments. Zack glanced back to Susan. She was not what he expected. Instead of being a nebulous figure, she was a pretty woman with soft looking honey-gold hair and grave gray eyes. She wasn't tall, reaching only to his shoulder. She kept her eyes on Danny, watching out for him, ready to spring to the rescue if needed.

She obviously loved him. That was one lucky little boy. Zack wondered how his own life might have been different if his parents had lived. If they had expressed the love he could see shining so clearly in Susan's expression.

Looking back at the little boy, Zack watched every move, every expression that crossed his son's face. Soon Zack would be healed and returning to the Middle East—or another project in a foreign land. For a few weeks he might get the chance to know Danny. He wished for him a better childhood than he had experienced.

"How long is your leave?" Susan asked.

"I have at least two more months." Two months to regain his strength and range of motion in his shoulder. He would do all the exercises the PT insisted upon. And walk the entire island of Manhattan every day if it meant full recovery. He didn't know what he'd do if he couldn't pass the company physical. Look for a new kind of work, he supposed.

"Wow, I love it when I get two weeks off in a row," Susan said.

"Yeah, vacation is far different from medical leave. When I had time off before, I'd visit different European countries."

"We'll be lucky to get to Europe once before Danny leaves home," she said wistfully.

"Who watches Danny when you're at work?" he asked. "I assume you work normal business hours." Careful, he warned himself. You shouldn't know anything about her. She needs to tell you herself or you'll give away the fact a detective investigated her.

"It's nine-to-five most of the time. Sometimes if something big is going on, I'll be on call for weekends or late night sessions. I do get three weeks vacation, but depending on what's going on in the world, I might not get it all at once," Susan said.

"Does Danny go to a child care center?" Zack

racked his brain for what limited knowledge he had about children. Some of the men who rotated into the field for the chance to make extra money had families. He'd listened to their tales of woe regarding children and child care while their wives worked. Most of the time he'd wandered away, seeking time alone. He hadn't related before.

"There is a lovely retired schoolteacher who lives in our building and watches him for me. It works out perfectly. She needs a bit of extra money to supplement her retirement pay. Danny gets to stay in our apartment with his own toys and books. She takes him for walks here in nice weather. I was so lucky to connect with her."

"Is it hard to get good child care?" Zack asked. There was so much he didn't know about this family. His foster mothers had all stayed at home to be there for the children. How did a single working parent manage?

"The hard part is leaving him for so many hours. I wish I could work nights and be home with him during the day. He's growing so fast. Edith gives me a report each day—how he liked preschool, when he napped, what he had for lunch, if any little friends from the neighborhood came to play. Things like that. It makes me feel more a part of his daily activities. But I miss the actual being there."

Zack nodded. He hadn't planned to get involved with Danny and his adoptive mother. But now that the opening had been made, Zack was intrigued with the mother of his child. He liked being with her. Would she consider expanding her circle of friends to let him in? He'd made the first step by inviting them to the zoo. He hoped Susan would accept. If not, he'd take one day at a time. He'd already attained more than he ever expected regarding his son.

Susan softly closed the door to Danny's room. He was already asleep. Amazing how he could go from full speed to instant sleep. She felt tired enough to fall in bed herself, but still had some cleaning to do and another load of laundry. She'd dust and vacuum the living room to give Danny a chance to wake up if he were going to. Then she'd quickly run the last basket of clothes to the laundry area. Danny would stay asleep all night and she'd only be gone a few moments. She normally took him with her, but this weekend would prove to be different. If she were going to spend the day at the zoo tomorrow, she needed to get a load done tonight. When he'd been younger, she had never left Danny alone, even to dash down to the laundry room. Now she felt better about leaving him for a few minutes. She carried a baby monitor that would alert her if he awoke before she returned. It wasn't ideal, but working single parents made do.

As she tidied the living room, she thought about Zack Morgan. How involved did she want to get with the man? He was only in New York to recover from injuries. Once he was fit again, he'd return to the Middle East and she'd likely never see him again.

It wasn't as if she were planning a long-term friendship. But he was at loose ends and she had not been so intrigued with a man since her husband. What harm could it do to go to the zoo? Danny would love it.

And she'd love to spend the day with Zack.

Guess that meant she'd decided to accept the invitation to the zoo. Danny would be thrilled when she told him. And it would be more fun for her to see it with another adult. Not that she didn't delight in her child. But sometimes she just wanted adult conversation.

When she returned from the laundry room, she'd call Zack and let him know they'd be happy to join him. Glancing at Tom's picture, she almost apologized. "It's not a date," she explained. "Just an outing with Danny. He seems nice." She wasn't telling her husband how she'd felt a surprising attraction to Zack. She wasn't interested in remarrying. How could she when Tom had been the love of her life? They had made such grand plans—all dust now that he was gone. She couldn't risk that kind of heartache again. Love made a person hostage to all the bad things that could happen.

"He's just a new acquaintance." Was she trying to convince herself or Tom?

"Maybe he'll become a friend. But he's only here

for a short time. Once his convalescence is up, he'll move on and I'll probably never see him again." The thought disappointed her.

As Susan was inserting her key into the lock upon her return from the laundry room, she heard the phone ringing. She rushed to answer it hoping it hadn't wakened Danny.

"Susan? This is Zack."

"Hi." She suddenly felt as shy as a schoolgirl when a boy called. "I was going to call you later." She took a breath. "Danny and I would love to go to the zoo with you. We can be ready before nine if you want to get an early start."

"Sounds good. I'll swing by your apartment about eight-thirty if that suits. Thought we'd take a cab rather than the subway. I could have rented a car for my stay, but the traffic is too much to deal with. And I'm not sure I could find parking anywhere."

She laughed. "That's one of the reasons I don't have one." Susan felt oddly nervous about the outing. It wasn't a date. She was merely going to the zoo with a new friend. And Danny would love it.

"Is Danny asleep?" Zack asked.

"Yes. We have a schedule. He does better with set times for things. So we're up every morning before seven. He eats lunch at noon and we usually eat dinner at the same time every evening. Then it's bath and bed by eight. Kids like routine."

She'd admit to a rampant curiosity about the man.

If she was planning to spend the day with him tomorrow, she could devote a bit of time tonight to get to know him better.

"So, tell me about working in the Middle East. What happened with the land mine?" Susan said, settling in on the sofa.

Zack began telling her about the land mine accident that had killed one construction worker and injured him. It had only been the heavy earth-mover that had shielded the other workers from harm.

Glossing over his time in the hospital, he soon turned the topic to heavy construction projects outside of the U.S. He told her about the heat and dryness of the desert. How for the most part the people were grateful for the improvements made especially when dams afforded water to heretofore barren land.

A buzzer sounded. Susan jumped. "My clothes are ready for the dryer," she explained. "I'll need to put them in." She hated to end the conversation. But if she waited too much longer, she'd have to stay up later than normal waiting for the clothes to dry. With a full day planned for Sunday, she wanted to get a good night's rest.

"How long does it take to do that? I can call back."

"Great. Give me ten minutes."

Zack hung up. The last forty minutes with Susan

on the phone had been unexpectedly nice. His friends were still on the job site. He knew no else in New York except the private detective he'd hired. She was easy to talk with, but he wished he'd learned more about Susan. She'd kept the conversation clearly on him, which made sense. She wanted to know more about him if she was seeing him in the morning.

He liked that. When he called her back, though, he'd make sure to ask her questions. He considered the possible complications of getting to know them while he was in the States. Would he develop a bond with his son? Or just know him these few weeks, and keep the knowledge of his paternity a secret? He wasn't sure how things would play out. But for the time being, he was content just to get to know Susan and Danny.

Ten minutes later he called again. She answered at the first ring. He pictured her rushing back to be there when he phoned. It was a nice feeling—and he wouldn't ask for confirmation. He wanted to hold on to those feelings.

"So tell me a bit about you—I dominated the conversation before," he said.

"That's because your life is more exciting. I fight the crowds to go to work. Come home and spend time with my child until he goes to bed. Stay up as long as I can keep awake then go to bed myself."

Zack tried to think like a man who knew nothing

about this woman, instead of knowing most of the facts of her life, thanks to the detective. "What do you do on weekends?"

"In nice weather I always take him to the park. It's our only grassy area. During the winter, we often visit museums so he can run around without getting cold. Sometimes in the summer we take a ride to the beach. Must sound pretty boring to a man who vacations in Europe."

"It depends on whom I'm doing it with. One appealing part of your lifestyle is the stability you have. I'm a nomad."

"By choice."

"Maybe."

"So by that do you mean you might be interested in settling down at some point?"

"I hadn't considered it. First I was going to make my mark on the world."

Zack didn't go into how he'd wanted to leave something behind to mark his being alive. He had no family so he built structures that would endure for decades and beyond. Now things had changed. Whether he ever let Susan and Danny know who he was, *he knew.* He had a son.

"It would be a change. But at some point surely you want a family?" she said.

"And if I die and they had to go into foster care? Too risky."

"Whoa, where did that come from?" she asked.

"It happened to my parents. I was raised in the foster care system in Chicago."

"Oh." Susan was taken aback. She remembered he said he didn't remember his mother. For some reason she'd thought his father was still alive.

"Hey, it's not a recent thing. I never knew either of my parents. I'm still in touch with one foster family," he said.

"That must have been tough." Susan wondered what Danny would do if something happened to her. She knew her mother would step in, but with her father in frail health, it would mean total turmoil for a long time. She couldn't bear the thought of not being there to see her son grow up.

"But what if you didn't die? What if you lived to be an old man and then had no children, no grand-children? Wouldn't that be worse?" she asked.

Zack tried to envision himself old, with lots of little children racing around yelling and laughing while he sat on some nebulous porch and watched. They would play in a big yard with old trees shading the grass. He would have his wife of many years beside him.

For a moment Zack wondered if he was losing it. The image popped and he was back in the small hotel room.

"I'll keep that under consideration," he said. "I called about the apartment sublet. It's still available and I'm going over on Monday to look at it," he said. "It's not close to your place."

"No, but a much better section of town. If they were subletting for longer, I might be tempted. But they want a short-term tenant. It sounds nice."

"I'll let you know if it works out."

They talked for another half hour. Susan finally said she had to get her laundry now that it was dry and gave Zack her address for the morning. He said good-night. After replacing the phone, he gazed out into the dark night. He'd see her again in a few hours. How did he feel about that?

Susan hadn't opened up to someone like Zack in years. She felt awkward now that the evening's companionable conversation had been broken. Riding down the small elevator, she wondered if she was being wise in going out with Zack. What if she grew attached—or worse, what if Danny did. He still searched for his father everywhere. She didn't want him doing the same for Zack if the man became part of their lives for the weeks he was recovering and then left. Little children didn't understand.

She and Tom had known from the first they were meant for each other. To think about another man felt odd. But she'd done it! She'd accepted a date for Sunday. She and Danny would spend several hours with Zack. Her heart gave an unexpected skip.

It was just for the day. Neither she nor Danny would grow too attached in such a short time.

When Zack rang the bell the next morning, Danny ran to the door. His mother had told him about the visit to the zoo at breakfast and he was raring to go. Flinging open the door he beamed up at Zack. Susan entered the living room in time to see her son open the door without even asking who was there. She was trying to instill some common sense in him, but he was too excited today to pay attention.

"Hey, there, Danny," Zack said, stooping down to smile at the small boy at his level. "Ready to go?"

"Yes!" Danny flung himself at Zack, his arms going around his neck. "The zoo is my bestest place. I love the elephants!"

Susan smiled at the stunned look on Zack's face. He hadn't planned on her exuberant son. "Danny, you're probably strangling Zack. Let go."

"No!" Tentatively Zack's arms came around the child and he hugged him gently. "He's okay, just excited, I think."

"You've nailed that. We're about ready." She put another bottle of water in the backpack and zipped it shut. By the time she donned her jacket and put Danny's on him, Zack had straightened to his full height and reached for the backpack.

"What do you have in here, bricks?" he asked, hefting it.

"No, just essentials." She raised her hand and began counting on her fingers. "Water, sunscreen, wet towelettes, snacks, cuddle blanket, dark glasses, wallet—"

"Cuddle blanket?" Zack asked, dumbfounded.

She grinned. "Danny still is comforted by a certain blanket when he gets tired or cranky. Usually he keeps it on his bed, but we take it with us on longer trips just in case. He likes to put it against his cheek and rub against it. I call it his cuddle blanket. Hopefully we'll leave the zoo before he starts getting tired. He can get really cranky."

"I expect I'll get tired long before he does," Zack said, slinging the backpack over one shoulder.

"I can carry it," Susan said. She remembered his brief recount of the land mine. She didn't expect him to carry her things.

"I'm okay with it. I didn't realize you had to tote so much on an outing," he said.

"This is nothing. When Danny was smaller, we had blankets and bottles and changes of clothes in addition to everything else. You can't imagine how much a small baby needs to travel."

Zack shook his head. "I'm learning every second."

"Danny, what did I tell you about this trip?"

He scrunched up his face for a moment then beamed at his mother. "Hold your hand in mine!"

"Good memory," she said and they exchanged a high-five.

As they walked down to the elevator, she said softly to Zack. "Of course I tell him that every time we leave the house. He ought to remember. But watch and see if I don't have to remind him at least a half dozen times."

"He seems to be a happy kid," Zack said.

"I hope so. I'm doing my best. It's hard being a single parent. My husband and I had always planned that I would stay at home when we had children. His death makes that impossible."

"Didn't he leave any insurance? Sorry, that's none of my business."

"That's okay. Tom left some, but I want that for fallback purposes, or for college. Do you know how expensive college is these days?"

Once at the street level, Susan insisted Danny hold her hand. They caught a cab and sat in the back, Danny in the middle.

"Are we at the zoo yet?" Danny asked at the first traffic light.

"No, it'll take a little longer to get there," Susan said. "We'll tell you when we arrive."

"Do you have zoos at your home?" Danny asked Zack.

"No. I haven't been to the zoo since I was a little boy like you."

"I'm glad we can go today."

Susan smiled at Zack. He looked bemused. She'd have to remember he wasn't used to being around kids and keep Danny from pestering him as he could do sometimes.

"My daddy goes to the zoo. Maybe he will be there today," Danny said, bouncing on the seat.

"No, Danny. Daddy's gone to heaven. He won't be at the zoo."

"I want my Daddy!" he said, kicking the back of the seat in front of him.

"You miss him so much, sweetie. I do, too. But he won't be at the zoo," she said softly. She glanced at Zack. "We'll really have to make sure he doesn't take off after some guy with light brown hair."

Zack nodded, realizing more and more each day how much he had missed. He hated the fact his son ached for another man. How could Alesia have kept this child from him? It hurt to think she'd given him away rather than tell Zack he was a father. He would have been home before the baby was born, and loved him from the first moment.

He'd accomplished his initial goal—discovered that his son was happy and healthy. Somewhere the goal had changed. Now he wanted to get to know the woman who was raising his son. See if he could help out in some way without being intrusive in their lives.

The cab arrived at the zoo. It had been years since Zack had been. One of his foster families had lived near the zoo in Chicago and they'd gone each summer the three years he'd lived with them. He had often wondered what the zoo looked like in winter, especially for African veldt animals in the snow of Chicago. Today the Bronx Zoo was warm and green. Families with children running were everywhere.

Susan stepped a bit closer to Zack and held Danny's hand. "I didn't expect such a crowd," she said. "It's only April."

"I didn't know what to expect. But after the rain, it's beautiful weather. I'm glad we came early. What do you want to see first?"

"Monkeys." She gave Danny's hand a swing. "I know he's descended from them."

The morning passed swiftly. Zack watched as Danny hung on every word his mother read about the animals. The child delighted in the Children's Zoo, exploring all the exhibits, and feeding the pygmy goats by hand.

"I'll pass," Zack said when Danny offered him a turn after a goat licked the boy's palm.

Susan laughed. "Definitely a wet wipes time. Before we eat, he needs to get his hands washed properly." She pulled out a wet towelette and wiped off Danny's hands. She offered one to Zack and took one herself. "No telling what we've touched so far," she said with a laugh. "Thanks for inviting us—we're having fun."

By the time they found a table at one of the eating

concessions, Susan was feeling more comfortable around Zack. He kept the conversation going without filling every moment of silence. Sometimes he just seemed to enjoy being in the day, looking around at the exhibits, studying the people. Probably a result of a near miss with the land mine. Had he always been like this, or had that event changed him in some ways? Curious, she watched him as they ate, wishing she knew more about him, but afraid to ask too much. She didn't want to give the wrong impression.

It was after one when they started lunch and by two o'clock, Danny was showing definite signs of flagging.

"I think we need to head for home," Susan said when Danny asked to be picked up for the third time. "You don't have to come with us. It'll be out of your way, I'm sure. Thanks for a great day. We've both enjoyed it."

"Actually I was thinking of returning myself. Here, let me carry him," Zack said, reaching out to take Danny. The boy weighed so little, but for Susan it would have been a greater burden.

The minute Danny put his arm around Zack's neck and lay his head against his shoulder, Zack wondered if he could ever let this child go again.

"Thanks. He's getting heavier by the day. I love him dearly, but he's almost too big to carry anymore." She looked a bit sad at the thought.

Zack wanted to erase the sadness from her eyes, but he didn't know how. He wanted her to be happy, have that love for her son be the only emotion he could detect.

"All kids grow up," he said inadequately.

"I know, but I didn't realize they'd grow so fast."

Zack carried Danny to the taxi, which he insisted they share. By the time they reached Susan's apartment building, the boy had fallen asleep and Zack carried him to his bed.

"Thanks so much," Susan said again as she pulled off Danny's shoes and covered him with a light blanket. "He'll remember this day for a long time."

"I will, too," Zack said, with a look at his son. And then he turned to leave the room. "Maybe you'll take pity on me another weekend and spend some time with me."

"We'll see," Susan said brightly. She had enjoyed the day more than she'd expected she would. But she was wary of getting too friendly. Yet he had done nothing toward pushing them closer. He was just a new acquaintance who hadn't met many people yet. He hadn't even offered a specific activity—just a nebulous spend time together.

She wasn't ready to date, she decided. When she was, she wanted to meet men who lived nearby, with steady jobs that didn't include the danger of a mine exploding.

After Zack left, Susan kept busy in the hopes of

keeping her disturbing thoughts at bay. Once she had caught up on chores and checked to make sure Danny was still asleep, Susan picked up a magazine and glanced through it, but her thoughts returned to Zack.

Somehow she needed to make it clear to him she wasn't looking for a new man in her life. She glanced at the closest picture of Tom. She had gotten used to being alone, though she still missed him like crazy. They should have had decades together. More children. She hated the thought of Danny being an only child. Yet she couldn't imagine getting married again.

Unless it was to someone like Zack, the thought crept in. He could almost make her forget Tom.

She frowned. Zack was nothing like Tom. She didn't want to even go there. He said he'd only be around for a few weeks, then he'd probably be off to some exotic country for another few years. The nomadic life might suit him, but it wouldn't suit her or a family.

Just then she heard Danny. She jumped up, magazine forgotten.

Monday morning Susan received a phone call at work from Edith Jordan. It was so rare, she was instantly concerned.

"Just a quick confirmation, my dear," Edith said. "We came to the park and Danny went to talk to a young man at a nearby bench. He said Zack took him to the zoo yesterday."

"Zack Morgan. And yes, he took us both to the zoo. Is there a problem?"

"Not at all, I just wanted to make sure he was a friend."

"Is Danny bothering him? I think Danny's taken a fancy to him." She took a deep breath and tried to think about it rationally. It would do no harm as long as her son didn't become too attached. She wouldn't want Danny to be upset when Zack left.

"Mr. Morgan doesn't seem to mind. I'll go and introduce myself and let him know he's free to tell Danny to stop if he gets too demanding," she said.

"Sounds like a plan. Make sure Danny knows just because Zack treated us to the zoo, it does not commit him to spending more time with him."

Susan hung up a moment later and shook her head. She knew Zack took long walks as part of his recuperating process. And sitting in the sunshine in a quiet park was probably just what he needed. For a moment she was envious. She wished she could sit in the park on such a nice day and enjoy the sunshine.

And spend time with Zack.

By Wednesday, Susan had managed to push thoughts of Zack to the back of her mind. Danny had been full of conversation on Monday evening about Zack and how high he'd pushed him on the swing and how he played catch with a ball. Checking with Edith, Susan had discovered Zack had stayed at the park the entire time Danny had been there that day. But he had not been there on Tuesday or Wednesday. Probably afraid Danny would enlist him as a playmate again, she thought.

After tucking Danny in bed, Susan debated going to bed early herself. It had been a stressful three days at work and she still had two days to go to the weekend. Maybe a long hot soak in the tub and then an early night would be the perfect ending to a not-so-perfect day.

Just then, the phone rang.

It was Zack. Susan was suddenly swept away with anticipation at the sound of his voice. Leaning back on the sofa, she smiled. "I heard about your big day on Monday," she said.

"At the park with Danny?"

"Right. I hope he wasn't a pest."

"Not at all. But it was humbling—he wore me out," Zack said in his husky voice.

Susan closed her eyes to better concentrate on that timbre.

"It took you two days to recover?" she teased. "Danny said you've been conspicuously absent from the park since then."

"Checking up on me?" The low murmur of his voice made her think of dark rooms, intimate settings, just the two of them together. She reached over and dimmed the lamp. Settling back in the cushions again she smiled at their silly talk. It had been a long time since she'd flirted with anyone.

"Hardly, but perhaps I should warn you, if you make an appearance in Danny's vicinity, I'm bound to hear about it, if not from Danny then from Edith."

"At least you know your baby-sitter is conscientious."

"Did she introduce herself?" Susan asked.

"And gave me the third degree. She knows more about me than my employer, I think. She's not a stand-in for your parents, by any chance?"

"Not at all. They've only met once."

"Both your parents are living?" he asked.

"Yes. In Florida. My dad isn't doing so well. But they love it there. Typical New Yorkers, flocking south for better weather."

"You have no yearning to join them? Florida beats New York winters."

"I'm not ready for that scene yet. There's too much to do in the city. Besides, I love skating at Rockefeller Center in winter. Seeing everything dusted in snow. Bet you didn't do much skating in the Middle East."

"Not where I worked, but I took winter vacations in Switzerland. Didn't do much skating, but the skiing's terrific."

"I guess you got to see a lot of Europe whenever you took leave," she said wistfully. One of the trips she and Tom had planned had been to see London, Paris and Rome. If she saved enough, maybe she and Danny could make that trip.

"I've spent more time in European cities than I ever expected to before I took the job. Now I've seen enough. It's time to explore my own country, once I'm up to par again."

"Danny wasn't too much for you, was he?"

"No. I had to fly down to D.C. to confer with some of my colleagues at the company. And to discuss the possibility of working in the States."

"And?"

"There's time yet to seriously consider the future. In the meantime, I'm going to enjoy my R&R and explore New York. As a native, maybe you could act as tour guide. What should I see first?"

There was so much to see. Her heart skipped a beat when she imagined herself showing Zack all her favorite places.

"Come by the U.N. one day and I'll give you a tour," she offered before she had really thought about it. Immediately she wished she could snatch back the words. Holding her breath, maybe he'd refuse. What was she doing inviting him to the place she worked?

"Wouldn't you be working?"

"I can always take a break." She did want him to come, see where she spent most of her day. No, she didn't.

She didn't know what she wanted.

"How about next Tuesday? Can we time the tour so we end at lunch? You can show me one of your favorite places and I'll treat," he asked.

"Sure. Come around ten. Depending on what's going on, I'll give you the deluxe tour." Susan's heart tripped faster. She was going to see Zack again. Just the two of them. Was she ready for this? Quickly she sought Tom's image in a photo—like a talisman. Zack was just a new acquaintance; she was simply being friendly. That's all there was to it. But even as she silently explained to Tom, she knew she was lying. This excitement at the thought of seeing Zack was more than being friendly.

"I'd like that," he said.

His deep voice sounded sexy, intimate. Susan shivered, suddenly reacting to the phone call in a very different manner. She usually spent her evenings alone. Now she had a connection with another adult. One who disturbed her senses in many ways and had her wondering more about him than she should be doing. This man made her feel more like a woman than she had in a long time. She had not died with her husband. Her emotions had been so concentrated in grief over the last two years, she had almost forgotten what other emotions felt like. This giddy anticipation set her nerves tingling.

"You didn't tell me what happened with the sublet," she said.

"After saying I could see it Monday, they sublet it on Sunday. I'm still at the hotel," Zack said.

"I'm sorry. I thought that was so promising."

"Sublets go fast, I was told. The company is paying the room, I'll just stay here for the time being."

"If I hear of something else, I'll let you know. It has to be easier in a home than a hotel."

"Not much difference to me. This beats the tent I have been living in for the last seven months. Hot and cold running water. Good food. Nice bed."

"You lived in a tent? You didn't mention that before." Susan was intrigued.

"It was only the last assignment." He began telling her of palatial housing, subpar housing and everything in between that they made do with when on assignment.

Susan remembered flat hunting with Tom. They'd had such fun picking out locations, arguing about floor plans, always with a future eye on a baby. The flat they had shared had been perfect. She was glad they'd had those years together. Glancing around, Susan knew Tom would have hated this place. It was small, dark and not at all what they'd chosen.

Which drew her up short. She was on her own now. She did the best she could and that was that. She was not going to sink into a pity party—especially when she had an intriguing man on the phone.

Zack was talking again. "After our outing on

Sunday I was hoping I could convince you and Danny to join me for dinner Friday night. I saw a pizza place close by you that has games for little kids. Does Danny like pizza?"

"I think little boys are born liking pizza. I know the restaurant you mean." She had rarely gone inside, but had ordered home delivery from the place several times.

"When do you get home from work?" Zack asked.

"Usually around five forty-five. Give me a few minutes to change. We can be ready to go around six-fifteen if that works." It was only pizza. Not a date. Men didn't take little kids on dates. The three of them would have a nice time together and it would be one less lonely night for both adults.

She'd see him the day after tomorrow. Susan didn't know whether to be delighted, or nervous. For once, looking at Tom's photograph didn't help.

CHAPTER THREE

ZACK hung up questioning if he was making a mistake continuing to see Susan. She was so unlike the women he'd dated over the last dozen years it made him wonder why she fascinated him. He was curious to know if she was a sleepyhead in the mornings or if she bound out of bed raring to face the day. Did she prefer coffee or tea? The one time he'd brought coffee, she'd drank it black. Did she like long walks? He was growing addicted to them. They made him feel better, even when he was tired afterward and needed to rest.

What were her routines? Her favorite activities? Did she like action movies? He and the men on the job sites loved fast-paced action films. He himself also enjoyed mysteries. Did Susan?

He frowned. He was getting too involved. Alesia had been the epitome of party girl—always out for a good time. The kind of woman he had liked to date. She had known the score—no commitment, no ties. His job over the last decade had not been suitable for any kind of long-term relationships.

But Susan was totally different. She was a forever kind of woman. And a devoted mother. Despite the difference, he liked her. Leaning against the pillows he gazed out the window at the minuscule view he had. Lights gleamed in the night. New York never slept. Rising, he went to stand by the window. He was too high up to hear more than a low hum of sound from the street. The lights glittered from towers and apartments and, far below, from cars zipping along.

He wondered what Susan was doing right now. He liked watching her expressions, she didn't seem to hide a thing. When she laughed, her whole face lit up. But, more often than not, he'd caught her looking sad.

She didn't deserve it. She and her husband should have had fifty or more years together. They'd adopted Danny in good faith. There were no guarantees on a happy ending in life, but he wished that for her. And Danny.

He walked to the small wet bar to get something to drink. The evening loomed long and lonely. He missed being on the job site where there was always work to be done or places to see. Guys to hang out with in the small bars that sprang up at all sites.

But even if he were back, he wasn't sure that would suit him now. The land mine had changed his perspective on what was important. Or was it learning he had a son? He popped open the can and drank. Some of each, probably.

Now that he'd met Susan and Danny, heard the love in her voice, Zack knew his son was better off than he would have been with Alesia. She had definitely not been the maternal type. If Alesia had told him before she had given birth, he would have come home to take his child. But would it have worked out for the baby? A single guy working in foreign locales? How would he have managed?

He knew Susan was a good mother. He could see Danny was doing fine. Another visit or two and then Zack would pull back. No sense getting too caught up in their lives. It would make it harder to leave when the time came.

Thursday evening when Susan returned home, Edith Jordan had started supper for her. Danny ran to meet her, waving an envelope.

"You got a note from my teacher," he said, jumping up and down.

Edith smiled as she gathered her things. "I think he believes that is good news."

"Are notes from teachers ever good news?" Susan asked as she slipped her finger beneath the flap and tore the envelope open.

"Not when I was teaching," Edith said. "Good night, Danny. See you tomorrow."

"'Kay," he replied, his eyes full of excitement as he watched his mother pull out the sheet of paper.

Edith remained by the door, her curiosity evident.

"They need repairs to some of the school rooms and to the playground equipment," Susan said as she quickly read the letter. "They are asking all parents to lend a hand. Apparently the school needs to come up to code on various things in order to keep going. If not, the city could shut them down."

"What kind of help do they want?" Edith asked.

"Either monetary donation or actually physical participation. Gee, what should I do, give them the extra seventeen dollars from my last paycheck, or go hammer nails, which I've never done, and thus probably could cost them more than any pittance I can give them."

"I'm sure there are other things you can do. You could paint. Or clean up trash. Do they have a list of things needed?"

"It says each room has a list of tasks and goods needed. Could you check for me when you take Danny in tomorrow?"

"Sure. Are major renovations planned?"

"It says the full scope is listed in the classrooms. Maybe I should go in late and take him myself to see what is needed."

"I'll see if they'll give me a copy of what they have. I think they should have sent all that information to the parents."

"Me, too, but they didn't."

Susan bid Edith good-night and went to change into casual attire. Soon she and Danny were sharing dinner. She delighted in hearing about his day. He knew some of the plans at the school because he talked about his classroom getting their bathroom fixed.

"I didn't know it was broken," she said.

"We have to use the bathroom in Mrs. O'Donald's room. So we have to tell our teacher early when we have to go potty," he said earnestly.

Susan nodded, thoughtful. She knew the building that the preschool operated from was old, but she'd never paid much attention to its state. If Edith couldn't get a list of tasks needed, she'd call herself Friday afternoon.

How she would manage another expense remained to be seen. She didn't want to take Danny out of preschool if she could help it. It provided his only interaction with other children except for when he played at the park. But her money only went so far.

Zack leaned against the wall in the hallway outside of Susan's flat Friday evening. Glancing at his watch, the second hand swept around another time. Zack had three more minutes until six-fifteen. He'd already been waiting for more than eight minutes. Once six o'clock had arrived, he'd been hard-pressed to contain his impatience. They were all going out to dinner together and he was very much looking forward to the experience.

It was close enough. He rang the doorbell.

A moment later he heard Susan calling for Danny

to wait. But the little boy was too exuberant. He flung open the door and beamed up at Zack.

"Hi!" Danny said. "We're going to eat pizza."

"I know," Zack said, smiling down at the child. He wanted to lift him up and hug him tightly. But caution was his watchword. He had to take this one step at a time.

Susan came hurrying into the entryway. "Danny! I told you not to open the door until I got here."

"It's Zack," Danny said, as if he'd known beforehand.

"You didn't know that. It could have been anyone."

"It's Zack."

She shook her head and grinned at Zack. "I don't want to scare him with tales about ax murderers, but good grief, he can't throw open the door every time someone knocks."

"Danny, next time, ask who is there before opening the door, okay, sport?" Zack said, stepping inside.

"'Kay," the little boy said running back to his room. "I'll get my sweatshirt."

Zack closed the door and looked at Susan. She wore slim slacks and a pretty green shirt. A sweater was slung over her shoulders. She looked a bit tired, but almost—happy to see him? A man could hope.

"I'm a bit early," he said.

"We're almost ready. Come in and sit down, I'll be right back." She fled down the hall after Danny.

Zack stood where he was, listening to the murmur of voices, watching as Danny ran back toward him a moment later. Love filled him for this small child he scarcely knew. Had things been different, Danny would be running toward him calling Daddy.

In less than two minutes they were in the elevator and on their way to dinner.

"This is such a nice treat," Susan said as they stepped into the early April evening. The shadows filled the canyons of the streets. The air was cooler than it had been. He watched as she took a deep breath and seemed to relax before his eyes.

"Tough week?" he asked, glancing from her to Danny. His son had taken his mother's hand and then reached for his. He looked up at Zack.

"Swing me," he said.

"What?"

"Oh, Danny, not now. Zack isn't up to that."

"What?" he asked again.

"Danny likes to swing between two adults who are holding his hands. But it's the last thing you need with a shoulder injury."

"I don't think swinging a little boy is going to put me back in hospital."

"Is one side stronger than another?" she asked.

He shrugged. It felt odd to have someone concerned about him. He'd been making his way alone for a long time.

"So what do I do?" he asked.

"Hold on tight and on three we'll swing him forward and then back. One time, that's all."

Danny shrieked with laughter with his swing. "Again!" he said.

"No, Danny. That's it." Susan was firm.

Danny shot her a frown, then spied several pigeons ahead of them. "Can I catch the birds?"

Susan laughed. "No, we are on our way to dinner. What would you do with them while we ate pizza?"

Zack looked at her. "He could catch them?"

"Of course not. Didn't you ever chase pigeons when you were a kid? He thinks he can catch them and I don't want to rain on his parade. Childhood is a fragile time. One to be cherished and to keep dreams alive as long as we can. We're a long time adults."

Zack wondered if she'd had dreams shattered before their time. Then he remembered her husband. She'd lost him a couple of years ago, decades before she should have. He didn't like thinking about it. He couldn't picture Susan married. Now that he knew her, he would always remember her as she was tonight.

She was young, pretty, personable. She'd most likely find another man to love. He wondered who had been the one unable to make babies? Susan or her husband. Perhaps another man would give her all the children she would want. Zack shook his head as if dislodging the image of her in the arms of another man. He watched the way she interacted with Danny. She'd be great with two or three more kids running around.

The pizza parlor was crowded. Families and teenagers on dates filled the space. There was a children's section at the back, with one lone table still empty.

"I'll grab that table," Susan said, nodding and urging Danny onward. They'd discussed what kind of pizzas they liked on the walk.

Zack ordered, getting a pitcher of cola and made it back to the table Susan had claimed. He glanced around. Danny was playing on one of the tot toys in the fake castle.

"He'll be entertained until the pizza arrives," Susan said, smiling at him when he set the pitcher down.

Slipping into the bench opposite her, he nodded. "I didn't realize how noisy it would be."

"Not a place for quiet discussions, that's for sure," she almost shouted. "But I like it. Lots of energy and fun. Did you go out for pizza a lot as a child?" she asked.

He shook his head. "Not until I was a teenager and bought my own. Many foster parents don't have lots of money. They spend more on the children than the state pays. Most of them do it for love. Which means money is generally tight."

"My mother is from an Italian family. She made pizza for us. I still think my mom makes the best pizza around. Next time she's up, I'll have her make you one. She loves to cook."

Zack nodded, wondering how soon that might be. That opened an entirely new line of thought. He hadn't thought about grandparents in a long time. Not knowing his own parents, of course he had not known any grandparents. Alesia had been estranged from her own parents, but surely that breach would have been healed with a grandchild? In the meantime, he was glad his son had grandparents from Susan.

Despite the noise and commotion constantly churning around them, Zack enjoyed the evening. He couldn't say he and Susan had a meaningful conversation—it was too noisy for that. Danny dashed back when the pizza was delivered to eat a few bites, then he was off again to play. The conversation was sporadic, Susan always keeping a careful watch on Danny.

"Does he know all those kids?" Zack asked, keeping an eye on the group of preschoolers enjoying the castle and tot toys.

"I don't recognize any of them. But kids that age love to play with others. They haven't started being shy or holding back. Having a child is a great way to meet others when moving into a new neighborhood."

"Tell me about the world's situation these days. No threats at the UN?" he asked. Much as he was enchanted with his son, he wanted to get to know Susan better, too. He'd never met anyone before whom he considered connected to. She'd forever be the woman who started his son on the road to maturity whatever the future held. But she was special in her own way. He wanted to learn everything he could, to bring out in the future and remember.

He liked watching her, the ways in which she gestured with her hands, the seriousness when she leaned forward to make a point, or the way her laughter rang out when she was amused. And though he knew she was talking to him, she continued to keep a careful eye on Danny. If he were injured or in trouble she'd be there in an instant.

Nothing untoward happened. Danny had fun, and surprisingly, so did Zack. The pitcher had long been empty and the pizza only a memory when he reluctantly suggested they start for home.

"Oh, I didn't realize how late it is. Danny usually goes to bed around eight. It's almost nine. I've had such fun," she said, almost in disbelief.

"That was the point, to have fun," Zack said, glad he hadn't been the only one enjoying himself.

"Then it worked! Help me corral my son?"

Danny resisted leaving, but Susan was firm. The walk back to the apartment wasn't as fun as the outbound one had been, due to a cranky child.

"Will he let me carry him?" Zack asked after a block.

"I guess he will. I can manage, though," Susan said.

"No! Zack carry me," Danny said when his mother reached for him.

"No problem," Zack said, swinging him up into his arms and holding him against his chest.

The heart was a funny thing. Zack didn't think it could get any larger, but it felt as if it were swelling with love for this child he was only just getting to know. Like must recognize like and he knew he would love Danny forever.

Susan tucked her hand in the crook of his elbow and they walked in silence for another block. It felt right, Zack thought. Like families he used to watch when he was a child. Longing for that special connection that joined father, mother and children, he felt the yearning again. Would he ever be part of such a family?

For a moment the thought of making Susan and Danny his family flashed into mind. He'd have his son and a loving mother for that son. There'd be family gatherings at holidays and birthdays. He'd belong as he never had before. And his son would be secure all his life in love from his father and the only mother he'd ever known.

It was a perfect solution.

Zack caught his breath. It would work. He could make it work. He already liked being with Susan. He thought she enjoyed being with him. Of course it was too early to discuss marriage. But with a special courtship, could they both come to want the same thing? Marriage?

He couldn't believe he even had such an idea. He'd never expected to marry. His work took him all over the world. And not to locations where he'd want a family. Maybe it was because he'd almost died in that land mine explosion that he had such an idea. Was it a pie-in-the-sky idea, or one with serious merit?

A woman wanted more than just a father for her fatherless son. She wanted to be wanted for herself.

Zack glanced down at Susan. She was pretty in ways that would last—not for her the flashy makeup and fleeting fashion statements his former girlfriend had embraced. She was nothing like Alesia. She would bring security to a marriage he doubted Alesia would ever have managed had she consented to marry him for their child's sake.

Susan glanced up and smiled. "Is he getting heavy?"

"Not at all. I've enjoyed tonight." More than he had expected.

"Me, too." She squeezed his arm slightly and looked away, a slight smile on her lips.

When they reached Susan's apartment, she invited him in.

"I'll put Danny to bed and we can have some coffee, if you like," she said, as she worked the key in the lock.

"Sounds great. I'd hate the evening to end so soon," he said. "I can help put him to bed."

"You don't need to."

"Want Zack," Danny mumbled, snuggling closer to the man who held him.

Susan laughed. "Okay, then. You have to get right into pjs and brush your teeth. No dawdling tonight, it's late."

"'Kay," he said.

Zack carried Danny into his bedroom and sat on the edge of the bed. Susan handed him a set of pajamas and Zack set Danny on his feet and helped him take off the sweatshirt and T-shirt he wore. It wasn't easy getting Danny to put on his pajama top; the child wanted to flop against him, already half asleep.

Finally he was ready and Zack followed the two of them to the bathroom to watch Danny brush his teeth. Leaning against the doorjamb, he enjoyed the routine Susan and Danny had with his son standing on the closed toilet lid and first brushing his teeth by himself, then with Susan helping.

"All done!" he sang out when Susan had him rinse his mouth.

He jumped from the toilet, straight for Zack. Only his quick reflexes had him catch his son before the boy landed on the floor.

"Danny, don't do that. It's dangerous," Susan scolded.

"Zack catched me," he said, beaming.

Zack vowed to always be there to catch his son if humanly possible.

"He's fearless," she said, shaking her head. "A little caution wouldn't hurt."

"Within reason," Zack said.

"You don't think I baby him too much, do you?" she asked uncertainly.

"Not that I can see. He's learning independence, and that's what parents want, right?" Zack asked, carrying Danny back to bed. He laid him down and covered him.

"Read me a story," Danny said, his eyes already drooping.

"Please," Susan added.

"Please."

Zack looked at the book Susan handed him. "If you read, I'll start the coffee."

Zack had never read a book to a child. He opened the first page noting there were only two sentences on most pages. It wouldn't take long to get through the book.

Even so, before he was halfway to the end, Danny fell asleep.

Zack leaned over and kissed his cheek. "Sleep well, little man." For several minutes, he just sat and gazed at this miracle—his son. His cheeks had healthy color, his eyelashes skimmed the top of the pudgy cheeks. His chest rose and fell, scarcely moving the sheet and light blanket. Time seemed to stand still.

Finally Zack rose and turned off the light. Did Susan close the door or leave it open? There was so much he still didn't know about his own son. He left it open and headed for the living room.

"Your timing is good—coffee's ready. I have some cookies, too, but nothing fancy for dessert," she said, bringing the coffee in on a tray. Macaroons were piled on a decorative plate. Napkins and mugs crowded in.

She had switched on two lamps in the room, and opened the curtains to let in the night lights from the city. It was cozy. A far cry from the rented places he'd lived in over the last decade. Most were only a place to get mail and eat and sleep. No photographs crowded tables, no paintings hung on the walls. No toys dotted the floor.

Susan had made a home for herself and Danny even in this small, old apartment. Something Zack envied.

If they married, he'd be included in her home. It was an odd feeling.

Glancing at the photographs of her husband, he wondered if he had a chance getting her to let go of the past and move ahead.

Whoa—he was getting way ahead of himself. He wasn't certain he was cut out for marriage. The first thing he'd have to change would be his job. He couldn't marry and expect a wife to live alone for two years at a time while he went off to build a bridge.

He'd never thought about settling down, making a family, buying a home.

Yet, why not? He'd wanted permanence when he'd been a child. He could make his own permanent arrangement. Buy a house with lots of yard space. Get a dog. Have cookouts in the backyard. Get to know his neighbors. Put down roots.

Would Susan want to leave the city? She said she loved it, but would she also be open to the idea of living in a house with a yard? It was something he'd yearned for when younger. If he stayed in the States, he could afford to buy the perfect house— suitable for a child and pets.

Susan watched as Zack's gaze roamed around her living room. She glanced around, trying to see it through his eyes. It reflected her personality and idea of home more than her late husband's. It was a comedown from the apartment she and Tom had shared, but she liked it. Did Zack like it? Or was it too feminine for him? He lived a rugged lifestyle— far different from what she liked.

"Do you miss being back at the job site? Will you go back to the same place?" she asked.

He leaned back against her sofa cushions and looked at her, his eyes narrowed in thought. "I do miss it. It's great work. I enjoy being part of the construction team bringing modern conveniences to a desperate place. But I think I'm ready for a change.

I want to set down roots and find a niche here that will bring me as much satisfaction. Maybe not right away, but I no longer see myself as a nomad for the rest of my days."

"And you once thought you would be all your life?" she asked.

He shrugged. "It's what I know. I had four foster homes growing up. By the time I was in high school, I knew not to become attached—there was always the possibility of being yanked to yet another one. This kind of life followed suit. The upside is the travel to countries I'd never have visited if I weren't doing this kind of work."

"So what changed?"

"Almost getting killed. Life is suddenly more precious than I expected. Things can change in a heartbeat. You and your husband had hopes for the future, he died. I don't plan to live in fear the rest of my life, but I don't plan to take it for granted, either."

She nodded, surprised to realize the crushing ache she used to feel when reminded of Tom's untimely death didn't threaten her tonight. She studied Zack for a moment. He looked tired, but virile and intriguing. She didn't usually relate to people as easily as she had him. Or invite them into her home. But it seemed right with Zack. Was it because he was recuperating from serious injuries and she felt compassion for all he'd been through?

No, she didn't feel a bit sorry for the man. The truth was he fascinated her. He lived abroad and worked at a job most men never even dreamed about. He'd faced danger and survived. On a purely physical level, he attracted her. His eyes were dreamy. His lips drew her attention again and again. Despite the recovery mode he was in, he was muscular and strong and made her feel special.

She blinked and looked away, seeking a picture of Tom. For once the connection she normally felt was missing. It was merely a colored photograph of a man she'd once known, loved and now mourned. Tom was gone.

Susan was not dead. And while they'd never discussed what the other should do if one died young, she knew Tom would have wanted her to explore all facets of life. To move on and find happiness elsewhere if she could. He had loved life, loved her and loved Danny. He would want the very best for them even if he couldn't provide it.

Did that mean getting to know someone else? Someone so different? Someone who made her feel like she was on the edge of something wonderful and thrilling—yet scary. She wasn't ready for that. She'd had a great marriage with Tom. It would be highly unlikely she'd find another man who could give her the same thing.

"Are you okay?" he asked.

She looked at him. "Yes, why?"

"Your expression looked almost scared."

"Sorry, I was thinking of something else." She glanced almost apologetically at Tom's picture then smiled at Zack. "Do have a cookie, or aren't macaroons ones you like?"

"I like them. I'm still full from pizza. That was fun tonight. I think Danny preferred the toys to the food, though."

"Yes, he loves to explore new things."

Zack reached out to place his cup on the coffee table and in doing so, knocked off an opened letter. He reached for it, glancing at it briefly.

"What's this?" he asked, putting it back on the table. "Danny's school needs repairs?"

"It's an old building, as is everything around this neighborhood. Last winter one of the storms found a weak spot in the roof and it leaked like crazy. The building inspectors came to check for mold. In doing the inspection, they found other items not up to current code. And the playground equipment is a bit antiquated. That letter is a call to parents for help."

"So what are you going to do?" he asked.

"I don't know yet. I'm not very handy. I don't think I've done more than hammer a nail into the wall to hang pictures. I did paint the kitchen. Guess I'll do what they assign me and hope for the best."

"Need more help?"

"You?"

"I'm at a loose end and going a bit crazy with in-activity. I'm not ready to return to work full-time. I need a doctor's release for the company first. But I could manage a bit of repair work."

"I can't ask you to do that."

"You're not asking, I'm volunteering."

She studied him for a moment. "I think that would be amazing. I doubt any of the parents have the kind of knowledge and experience you have. But it's strictly volunteer."

Zack smiled. "I know that, Susan. I'd be happy to help."

"Wow. Great. I'll let them know Tuesday when Danny goes again. There's a planning meeting on Wednesday evening and the projects begin Saturday. Are you sure?"

Zack nodded.

"Thank you. Do you remember where the pre-school is?"

"Just a few blocks from here."

"Yes. I was going to walk over after dinner on Wednesday. If you want to come here for dinner first, we can go together."

"Sounds like a plan. Will Danny be coming?"

"No, Edith is going to watch him. I really appre-ciate this, Zack. It'll really help the school."

"No problem. As I said, I could use the activity." He rose. "I think I should be heading out. It's getting late."

Susan nodded and put down her cup. Standing, she led the way to the door. "Thanks again for taking us to dinner. I know Danny loved it."

"Thanks for going with me," he said. He leaned over and brushed his lips against hers.

Susan caught her breath. For a moment Zack's eyes met hers, then he leaned in again, reaching for her this time, pulling her into his embrace. When his lips met hers, she closed her eyes and kissed him back.

She didn't know Zack well, but the attraction she'd been fighting surged to the front. His mouth moved against hers, his arms held her securely. She leaned in, wanting more. Thrilled at the sensations that swept through her, she opened her lips to return his kiss. When he deepened the embrace, she felt herself spinning through space tingling with desire.

Before she could begin to think coherently, he pulled back a little and then brushed her damp lips with his thumb. Looking into his dark eyes, she could see wonder, desire and something else in them. She had a million questions, felt a dozen different emotions. But knew she wanted more from this man. He ignited her senses, filled her with a delight she hadn't experienced in a long time.

"I really enjoyed tonight," she said. She wanted to say more, but felt suddenly uncertain. Was he kissing her because he hadn't been with a woman in a long time? She couldn't bear it if that were the case. Susan hoped he had meant more by it. She wanted to know more about Zack. Was she being susceptible to the first man she'd been attracted to since Tom's death, or was there truly something special about Zack himself?

He dropped his hands and stepped to the door. Opening it, he turned and looked at her. Susan felt her heart skip a beat at the look in those dark eyes.

"Want to go on a picnic with me to Central Park tomorrow?"

"Danny?"

"Always included," he said.

"We'd love to." How had she lucked out in finding a man who would include her son whenever he saw her?

CHAPTER FOUR

SUSAN called her mother for their weekly chat early on Saturday morning. As usual, she asked after her father first.

"He's going strong and I plan to keep him that way for a long time!" Amelia Molina said. "How is that precious boy of ours?"

"Danny's doing fine. He still loves preschool and now that the weather allows him to get to the park more often, he's in heaven. He loves the spiral slide best."

"Are you going to the park today?" her mother asked.

"Actually we're going on a picnic to Central Park," Susan said. She realized she hadn't told her parents about meeting Zack. There was not much to say.

"With that friend of yours who has a child?" her mother asked.

"Actually it's with someone I met recently. He's on leave right now and trying to see as much of New York as he can."

"He?" Her mother almost pounced on the word.

"Zack Morgan." She hadn't told her parents about Zack's role when Danny had run after a stranger thinking it was Tom. Now it seemed too late. "Someone I met because of preschool." That was the truth, just not all of it.

"An older man?" her mother asked.

"Not so old—just a few years older than I am." Susan hadn't considered how old Zack was. "He's been working in the Middle East the last few years."

"Ah."

"What does that mean?"

"I didn't realize you had started dating again. It's a good thing, honey."

"Mom, we're not dating. We've hardly spent any time together and Danny is always with us. I don't consider that dating."

"He likes Danny?"

"Zack seems to like him very much." Susan remembered how he'd carried Danny home from pizza and tucked him into bed. "And I'd say Danny likes him a lot. He insisted Zack read him his book last night at bedtime." Now that she thought about it, Danny had not looked at every man in the pizza place to see if he were Tom. Maybe meeting Zack had been a good thing.

"This Zack was there last night?"

"Mom, we went to pizza. He walked us home, read Danny a book and that's all. Don't go making more of this than warranted." She didn't see any reason to tell her mother about that kiss. The kiss that had kept her awake half the night, and dreaming X-rated dreams the other half.

"I want you to be happy, honey. We all miss Tom. It's dreadful his dying so young. But you need not be a widow all your life. If you find happiness with another man, Tom would never have stood in your way. Clinging to the past won't bring him back, honey."

"I know." She looked at the closest picture. Tom was smiling into the camera. For a moment she felt the happiness in that day. He had loved life. He would want her to embrace it as well. But it was hard. She missed him so much. She didn't know how to move on.

Could she with Zack?

Too early to tell. Though she had been thinking about him a lot. And about the feelings she was coming to expect when around him—excitement, anticipation, desire.

"So your father and I should come up to meet Zack," her mother said.

"No, you should not. If anything develops, I'll let you know. For the moment, he's just a lonely guy who wants some companionship when he goes sightseeing. We went to the zoo last week."

"Sounds to me like it's more than being acquaint-ances, but I'll wait for you to tell me if we need to come up. Is Danny around? I'd love to talk with him. Poppa wants to talk to him as well. Then your father will want to talk to you."

Susan called Danny and stayed nearby listening to his side of the conversation. At one point she almost interrupted. To hear Danny talk, Zack was the center of his world. She hoped her parents weren't getting the wrong idea. Or getting their hopes up. She knew her mother felt a woman was incomplete without a man. Not that she couldn't do whatever she wanted, but she loved being married and thought that should be the goal of every woman on the planet.

Susan wasn't sure she would ever go down that road again. She and Tom had shared something special. Could she ever find that a second time? What if she married and found she continued to miss Tom. Or compared a new husband to Tom. Or worse fell in love and lost him again.

"Okay." Danny turned and handed her the phone. "Poppa wants to talk to you."

"Hi, Dad."

"How's my best girl?"

"Mom must not be nearby," Susan said.

He laughed. "She's right here, but knows you are my best girl. Danny talked of nothing but this Zack. What do you know about the man?"

Susan spent a couple of minutes filling in her father with what limited information she had on

Zack. Then she changed the subject and asked after her dad's bingo nights.

When the conversation ended, Susan couldn't say she was sorry. She needed to be careful about what she said in the next phone call with her parents. She didn't want them projecting their own desires for her future on to Danny.

As she got Danny ready for their picnic, she wondered if she should be so quick to accept all Zack's invitations. She'd been happy they included Danny. Her little boy still missed his father, even two years later. She ached for him and knew he was too young to fully understand his daddy was never coming home.

But he was not too young to bond with another male. She wasn't changing one heartache for another, was she?

When Zack arrived and knocked, Danny ran to the door. "Who is it?" he yelled, then quickly opened the door.

"Hi, Zack," he said, smiling up at the man.

"You didn't give me time to answer," Zack said, reaching out to tousle the little boy's hair. "Next time let me tell you who is at the door before you open it, okay?"

"'Kay," Danny said. "Mommy, Zack's here."

"So I see," Susan said, coming into the tiny hall. She felt breathless with anticipation. For one crazy moment she wished he'd reach out and kiss her senseless. But not in front of Danny. And maybe never again. She needed to keep her head straight.

The day was lovely. A slight breeze blew from the west, keeping the temperatures down, but the sunshine more than made up for it. Danny had only been to Central Park a few times. When they arrived and he saw the vast expanse of lawn, he was awed.

"Most green I've seen in years," Zack said, surveying the same expanse.

"I bet it's really brown in the desert," Susan said. She was prepared to enjoy the day and not remember their kiss. And she refused to wish for more.

Or she tried to. As the morning wore on, she found herself looking at Zack's mouth more and more, remembering the tingling awareness that had swept through her when he had fastened his lips against hers. Darn it, she did want another kiss. Just to see if the first had been a fluke.

And if it hadn't? She didn't know what she'd do. She hardly knew him. They had so little in common. He worked thousands of miles away. How could she expect some kind of long-term relationship? Yet he was the most exciting man she knew. There was so much to discover, and enjoy in the process.

They saw the Alice in Wonderland sculpture and rode the carousel several times to Danny's delight. Susan laughed more than she had in months. Zack had a way of making the day special and fun. Danny was enchanted to have the man stoop down and talk to him on his level. More than once he leaned against Zack's shoulder when he explained something to the boy. And he had stopped looking at other men trying to find Tom.

Shortly after noon Zack pointed to a sheltered spot and asked if they'd like to have the picnic there.

Susan nodded as Danny ran ahead and then turned to wait for them.

Zack had toted a large canvas bag around all morning and now he began to unpack it

"I bought fried chicken, crusty bread and chocolate milk," he said, taking first a blanket from the bag then a small, soft sided cooler.

"Something we'll all like," she said, touched he'd gone to such trouble.

Lunch proved to be fun. They were still within range of the carousel music so when conversation ebbed and flowed, the music filled the silence.

When they finished, Zack leaned back and closed his eyes.

"The sun feels good. Warm, not blazing like the heat of Arabia."

"Time for everyone to rest," Susan said, grabbing Danny when he jumped up and was ready to run.

"I'm not tired," he protested.

"Well I am and so is Zack."

"Lie down here by me, Danny, and we'll look at the clouds," Zack invited.

Susan glanced up. There were only a couple of small puffy white clouds in the sky. Danny lay down right beside Zack.

"Now we look at the clouds and see what pictures we can see," Zack said.

"Where are pictures?" Danny asked, looking around.

Zack glanced over at Susan. "Aren't you joining us?" he asked.

She scooted down until she lay beside her son. Smiling she studied one cloud, pointing it to Danny. "I see a rabbit," she said.

Soon Danny caught on and the three of them found the most outlandish pictures in the few drifting clouds. Before long Danny fell asleep and when Susan glanced over, Zack looked as if he had as well. She felt such a feeling of well-being. It was fun to shed responsibilities for a few hours and just enjoy herself. She closed her eyes and let the sun warm her.

She awoke with a start a short time later. Danny was still asleep, but Zack sat on the edge of the blanket, his gaze a million miles away.

"Sorry, I didn't mean to fall asleep," she said, sitting up.

"I dozed a bit myself." He turned to look at her. "Danny's not going to get sunburned, is he?"

"I put on sunscreen this morning, but let's rig up some shade." She moved the canvas bag so it was beside her son, then took off her sweater to make a lean-to shade for him.

"You won't get cold?" Zack asked.

"I'm warm now. If it gets cooler, I'll wake him up. But for now the nap is good for him. Keeps him from being cranky."

"How do you manage all you do with a rambunctious four-year-old?" Zack asked.

"I didn't have to work when he was younger. Edith has been a lifesaver since Tom died. It would be so much harder if I didn't have her to help me."

"It would be better if he had a parent at home all day."

"That was our plan. Only Tom got killed and so I had to go to plan B. Or maybe it was plan C, because we never even considered one of us dying before Danny grew up. I had planned to stay home at least until he started school. I miss so much. He changes every day. Edith takes pictures for me and my parents. I mail a bunch out every few weeks so they'll keep connected. But it's not the same."

Zack nodded.

"I guess you don't have any photographs of you as a child," she said thoughtfully.

"Actually I do have one album in storage. The foster parents took pictures at birthdays and Christmas. And I have my senior high school yearbook. The past doesn't mean so much to me—it's the future I look forward to."

She could understand the past didn't hold special memories for Zack. It was too sad that children had to grow up that way. "I should have brought a camera today, but I don't have any film. I need to pick some up."

"I took pictures of different bases, not many but enough so I can remember them down through the years," Zack said slowly. "Before and after shots, and some as the work progressed."

They seemed a poor substitute for family photos.

"Do you have access to them? I'd love to see them sometime," she said. It would give her more information, help understand him better perhaps.

"So one night we'll share photo albums. I'm glad you came with me today."

"I've enjoyed myself." Once again Susan's glance dropped to Zack's mouth. She quickly looked away.

Zack felt her look like a physical touch. She'd done that several times today; looked at his mouth and then quickly looked away. Was she remembering their kiss? He'd thought of it ever since last night. He was coming to really like this mother to his son.

He had also enjoyed today. Danny seemed to feel comfortable around him. He expected more resistance. Would it take long to win his complete confidence and trust? Could he at some point in the future reveal who he really was?

The longer Zack was around the boy, the more he

wanted to be. This was his son, his own flesh and blood. So many things he'd wished for as a child he could give to this boy. He never wanted anything bad to happen to him. What if Susan was killed unexpectedly like her husband? Who would take care of Danny? Had she made provisions? Or was she hoping she never needed another plan B?

He hoped she never did.

Zack watched his son nap. He was so trusting and loving and full of life. Had Zack once been like that? Before circumstances had taught him to be wary of bonds that could be shredded in a heartbeat when he was reassigned a different family. He'd sometime imagined his parents had lived and been searching for him. And one day found him.

He wondered if Danny had been told he was adopted? If not, would Susan tell him when he was older? What kind of questions would he have about his birth parents? Zack never wanted him to think his father had let him down. Family ties were important.

He was happy Danny had been adopted by the Johnsons. Susan was a great mom, just like he would have liked as a boy. Danny was lucky despite the heartache of the only father he knew dying.

"I'm thirsty," Danny said.

"You're awake," Susan said, moving her sweater. "There's another bottle of water."

Zack watched as Danny drank almost half the

contents and then jumped up. "Where are we going now?" he asked.

"I thought we'd take a carriage ride later," Zack said.

"Let's go!" Danny said, excited.

"Wait until we pack up," Susan said.

Danny began running.

Zack rose, ready to give chase if needed. "Danny," he called.

The little boy stopped and turned.

Zack crooked his finger. When Danny slowly walked back, he said, "We have to pack up as your mother said. You're growing up now, you need to take responsibility for some chores you can handle."

Danny's eyes got big. "I have respons'bility?"

"Yes. Right now, you can take the trash to that can over there. Then come right back." Zack handed him a small bunch of napkins and foil.

Susan watched, bemused, as Danny carefully held the trash in both hands and took it to the trash can. Smiling, he ran back.

"Good job," Zack said. He glanced at Susan who was studying him.

"Did I overstep a boundary?" he asked.

"Not at all. I think I'm keeping him a baby too long. But he's growing fast and while I love each stage, I really cherished the baby time."

"I think I can understand that, but a child needs to push boundaries. That's how they grow and learn."

"So you know about kids?" she teased gently.

"Only from growing up around them," he said gravely. "I had a lot of different families to compare, and to see what worked and what didn't." At least that part of his childhood had been beneficial—helping him formulate his own code of behavior, and the desires he had for a family of his own. He'd almost forgotten the days he'd sat on a lonely park swing, dreaming of how things would be when he had a family. Work over the last decade had demanded all his focus.

Now that he was in an enforced resting period, he had time to think. And plan for a future that possibly included his son in some way. And Susan. He glanced at her, taking a good long look. Her hair was slightly disheveled by the nap and the breeze. Her cheeks were glowing and her eyes sparkled. He felt a tug on his heart. She was open and fresh and sexy as any woman he knew. If it weren't for Danny, and they weren't in the middle of Central Park, he'd draw her into his arms again and kiss her. Last night had been chancy; now all he could think about was kissing Susan again.

"I welcome all suggestions," she said as they began walking in the lush grass. "Parenting does not come with a handbook. Being a solo parent isn't easy. No one to bounce ideas off of, or discuss serious situations."

"Your parents don't help?" He tried to focus.

Forget kissing her anytime soon. But sooner or later they'd be alone.

"To a degree. But I don't want them to feel they have to put their lives on hold while I struggle with mine. Their living so far away doesn't make matters easier. And Tom's mother is in bad health, lives in an assisted-care facility in California. His dad died before we were married. So Edith is really a huge help. A member of our family, so to speak. Anyway, enough about me. What do you want to do next?"

Spend more time with you, was the immediate involuntary thought. Zack glanced down at Susan as she called to Danny to come back to walk with them. He felt a small spurt of contentment. She was having a good time because he'd invited her on this picnic. Did he have the capacity to give her a good time always?

"I brought a ball. Would Danny like to play catch?" Zack asked.

She laughed. "He'd love it. But don't expect any coordination yet. If you lob it gently right to him, he'll catch it one time out of three. He's pretty good at throwing," Susan said. "Danny! Want to play catch?"

"Yes!" He ran back to them, his eyes shining. "Did you bring a ball?"

"I did," Zack said, reaching into the bag and pulling out a small, soft ball.

"Thank you!" Danny said, hugging Zack's leg.

The three of them played catch for as long as

Danny was interested. Then Zack gave him the ball and sat on the grass to watch as Danny threw it high in the air and tried to catch it. His lack of success didn't seem to dim his enjoyment.

Susan sat beside Zack. "You seem to know exactly how to entertain a little boy. Remarkable since you haven't had much to do with children lately."

"I was a boy once."

"Did your foster parents play ball?"

He shrugged. "The Zumwalts did. George Zumwalt was big on bonding, on giving the children they watched lots of experiences and fun times."

"What happened to him?"

"He died unexpectedly of a heart attack when he was only forty-three," Zack said. He remembered the pain of that loss. His wife had not been able to continue in the foster care program and Zack and the two other foster children had been split up and sent to new homes.

"I'm sorry."

"Yeah, I was, too."

Susan looked at Danny. "As time goes on, Danny will remember less and less about his father. I wonder even now how much he remembers and how much he knows from the stories I tell. I guess I'm one of the lucky ones—both my parents are still living."

"You are. One day you'll marry again and that man will be a role model for your son. He will have parents and Danny would have even more grandparents," he said.

Susan shrugged. "I don't know. I loved Tom so much. I still can't believe he's gone." She rubbed her chest. "The ache just doesn't seem to go away."

"There are other reasons to marry. To form a family. For companionship."

"I know. But somehow without love, I just don't think it would work. It's hard enough to be tied in a marriage when bad things happen. Disappointments. Frustrations. If there's no bond of love, how would two people survive all that life throws at them?"

Zack leaned closer, reaching out to catch her hand in his and threading his fingers through hers.

"By working together through whatever hardship comes. Even if deep love doesn't come, there could be affection and respect and liking. Would that be enough?"

Susan stared into his eyes. Zack could see the hesitation. He leaned back and squeezed her hand gently, letting her go. He was pushing too fast.

"I'm a fine one to talk. I've never married."

Susan gazed at her hand, clinching it into a fist.

Zack couldn't expect Susan to give him all the love her first husband had. But he would always be a devoted husband and always love Danny. That should count for something. Could she see it that way?

They walked to where the carriages queued up. Zack paid as Susan lifted Danny into the white carriage and then climbed up after him. Danny was excited with the prospect and asked if he could ride the horse.

"No. The horse's job is to pull the carriage. You can watch the driver and maybe one day you'll want to drive a carriage," Susan said as Zack joined them on the bench seat.

Slowly the horse started off. Danny bounced on the seat with excitement.

Zack stretched his arm on the back of the seat, his hand just inches away from her shoulders. Susan tried to relax and enjoy the ride, but her senses were revved up and attuned to Zack's every move. It had been a long time since she'd felt this way around a man. Not since Tom.

They left for home after the carriage ride. Danny wanted Zack to come in and play with him.

"Not today, sport. Zack's spent enough time with us. He has to do things on his own," she said, with a quick smile at Zack. It wasn't Zack who needed time alone, it was her. Her heart had kicked up a notch when he'd taken her hand this afternoon. She'd wanted to recapture his when they walked to the taxi stand in the Park, but had been too uncertain of how he'd take it.

She never wanted him to think she was some lonely widow looking for a man any place she could find him. Was her mother right? Did a woman need a man? She hoped not, for her sake.

"Thanks again for the picnic. I can't remember the last one I went on," she said to Zack in the elevator as it rose to her floor.

"Thank you for coming. A picnic for one just wouldn't have been the same."

"I guess not." She stepped off when the elevator reached her floor and the doors opened. Not Danny.

"I could come to your house and play," he told Zack, gazing up at the tall man.

"Danny, no more today. Come along." For a moment Susan was tempted to say the same thing. Only the play she had in mind wouldn't be for children, but two adults.

Shocked at her thoughts, she reached for Danny and urged him from the elevator. She knew people couldn't read minds, but she had to clamp down on her emotions before Zack picked up an inkling of what she was feeling.

She marched to her front door, resolutely refusing to turn to watch as Zack was enclosed behind the doors of the elevator and whisked away.

"Get a grip," she said softly as she fumbled with the key in the lock.

"What?" Danny asked.

"Nothing. Let's wash our hands and have some juice, then you can play in your room for a while."

Zack's talk of marriage had been sad. Wasn't he

looking for love? She thought hc was expecting too little. She and Tom had had a wonderful marriage. They'd loved the same activities, same movies. They'd never ran out of things to talk about. Especially after a long day at the office when he came home and wanted to know every detail of Danny's day. That first year they had Danny had been especially amazing. She longed for that close tie again. Maybe her mother was right: she did need another husband.

But her expectations for a mate seemed higher than Zack's. Maybe because she came from a loving family and he had none. Or maybe because of a myriad of other reasons. Whatever—was she softening in her no-more-marriage view? Was it time to let go?

It was too hard. She wanted to cling to all they'd had for as long as she could. Her marriage to Tom had been the best time of her life, and she hated to know it was gone. If she could just talk to him once more, spend an afternoon together. She had not properly cherished their time together, had taken it for granted and in an instant it had vanished. Could she ever move on, trust in the future enough to take a chance with another man? She didn't think she could live through the heartache of losing a husband again.

Yet, did she want to live a lonely life from now until she was old and gray? That would mean possibly passing up a happy future simply to cling to the past. That sounded equally unacceptable. She didn't like feeling so confused.

It was just too hard.

CHAPTER FIVE

SUNDAY it rained.

Susan was grumpy because of lack of sleep. She had tossed and turned all night, thinking about Zack. She wouldn't settle for a companion role, but could see the appeal to a man who might not know much about love. Just to have someone to make a family with would be important to him.

Once she had fallen asleep, she'd dreamed about Zack. She couldn't escape the man!

Danny was fussy. He wanted to go to the park, but Susan had said no. Summer rain could be fun to walk through, but it was still early spring and cold outside.

By ten o'clock, Danny had tired of playing in his room, didn't want to watch a DVD and yelled at Susan that he wanted Zack to play with.

She put him on time-out for five minutes for yelling at her, but felt sorry for the little guy. She wouldn't mind Zack stopping by to visit herself.

In desperation, Susan bundled him up and they

went to the market. The closest one didn't have all the things she wanted, but she bought two full bags of groceries, including chocolate chips. She and Danny could bake cookies when they got home. It beat having him drive her crazy.

"Hello, Susan, dear," Edith said, coming around the end of the aisle and seeing the Johnsons.

"Edith, how are you?" Susan looked sharply at her neighbor and baby-sitter. The older woman looked pale.

"Not feeling so well. I'm sure I'll bounce back and be right as rain tomorrow. Oh, dear," she said with a slight grimace. "Rain today isn't so right."

"I wish you'd told me you needed something from the store—it would have saved you coming out in this nasty weather," Susan said. "Can I help you home with your things?"

"I bought plenty of soup. Just in case. If I'm not better in the morning, you may need to make other arrangements for Danny. I don't want him to get sick."

"Don't worry about that. You concentrate on getting well. Let me help."

Susan carried the bag with Edith's soup cans, plus her own items. Danny was subdued around her and Susan hoped he was being attentive to her situation and not coming down with something himself.

"Thank you, dear," Edith said when they reached her apartment. "I'll just put the food away and then lie down."

"No, you go lie down now. I'll put things away, and make you some of this soup. When did you eat last?"

"I couldn't eat anything earlier. A small cup of soup does sound nice about now," the older woman said, taking off her raincoat and laying it across the back of her sofa.

Susan knew she was sick. Edith was fastidious about caring for her things. Normally she'd never put a wet raincoat over her sofa.

Susan hung it up to dry in the kitchen and quickly put away the few items Edith had purchased. She then prepared a cup of soup for her and carried it into her bedroom.

"Here you go," she said. Edith had already changed into a nightgown and was beneath her covers.

"Thank you. I shall be fine in short order," the older woman said. She still looked pale.

"Maybe not. Even if you are, you won't want to watch Danny tomorrow. I'll see if I can find another sitter, or stay home with him myself."

The fact her child-care provider didn't argue showed Susan how sick she truly was.

"Do you need anything else?" Susan asked, resisting the urge to feel her forehead to see if she had a fever.

"I'll be fine."

"Well, I'll check back later."

"Thank you, Susan, you run along now." Her lids

were already dropping. Susan waited long enough for her to finish the soup and took the cup.

"You were a good boy, Danny," she said when she entered the kitchen and found her son gazing out the rain drenched window. She was proud of how well he could behave when the chips were down.

"Is Edith going to die?" he asked, looking worried.

"No, honey, not for a long, long time. She's just a little sick. Come on, we'll head for home and make our cookies. We'll come back down in a little while to check on her, okay?"

"'Kay," he said, climbing down from the chair and looking closely at Susan.

"You won't get sick, will you, Mommy?"

"I won't. At least I hope neither one of us does. Come on, tiptoe so we don't disturb Edith."

A couple of hours later several batches of cookies cooled on wire racks on her counter. Susan and Danny surveyed them proudly.

"I helped," Danny said.

"Yes, you did. You were a good helper."

"Can we give some to Zack? I bet he doesn't have chocolate chip cookies at his house," Danny said.

"That would be a good idea." And a good excuse to see him, just for a moment. She had his phone number. Would he like them to come and bring him cookies? Probably taking a child to a hotel room wasn't the wisest move. Maybe he was tired enough of his hotel he'd relish the walk over.

Glancing out the window, she saw the rain had stopped. For how long, she wasn't sure. It was still gray and overcast.

"And we can give some cookies to Edith," he added.

"I'm not sure she'll be up to cookies, but we'll take her some just in case," Susan said.

They carefully packed two plates with cookies. Heading out to check on Edith, Susan gave the plate to Danny to carry. He solemnly walked to the elevator and waited for her to press the button.

Edith had grown worse. Admonishing Danny to sit on the sofa and not touch anything, Susan prepared Edith some more soup and brought her a warm washcloth to freshen up. The woman had a high fever and Susan made sure she had aspirin before giving her the soup.

"Shall I call a doctor?"

"No. Don't get near me, Susan. You need to stay well for Danny. I'll ride this out and be better before you know it. Go on now. I thank you for stopping by."

"When you finish the soup," Susan said. "We'll be quiet in the living room. But I want to make sure you're holding it down before we leave."

"I'll be fine," the older woman said, but she sat up against the pillows Susan plumped up for her and began to sip the soup.

It was more than a half hour later when Susan and Danny left. Edith had fallen asleep again. Susan knew the older woman had no one else, so vowed she'd check in on her each day at least once or twice.

When she returned to her apartment, she gave way to impulse and called Zack.

"Morgan," he answered. Her heart began pounding at the sound of his voice.

"Hi. Miserable day, isn't it?"

"I like it. I walked to a coffee shop this morning in the rain. When you live in a desert most of the time, rain is a treat."

"It's cold and damp and dreary," she countered.

"But rain keeps that grass in Central Park green. And washes the air. It is clean and crisp outside."

"So, want to take another walk in that crisp, clean air?" she asked.

"To?"

"My place. Danny and I baked chocolate chip cookies this morning. I wish it was nice enough to take him to the park. That would burn off some of his energy. Be prepared, if you come over, you'll have to participate in entertaining a rambunctious kid." She was talking too fast, as if she didn't leave an opening for him, he couldn't refuse.

She hoped he'd want to come over. She wanted to see him.

"Sounds like a plan. I love chocolate chip cookies. I don't think I've had homemade ones since I was a kid. I can be there in a half hour."

"We'll be here." She hung up feeling breathless with anticipation. He was coming over. Granted, Danny would be a perfect chaperone. But she didn't care; she'd get to see Zack again. And then it was only a couple of days until he came to see where she worked. And then there was the school meeting on Wednesday evening.

She could use the time until Zack arrived to line up a baby-sitter for a couple of days.

It was midafternoon by the time Zack arrived.

"We made cookies!" Danny announced, beaming up at him.

"So you did. Chocolate chip, my favorite."

"Come on," Danny said, racing for the kitchen.

Susan laughed, bubbling with happiness. She was glad he'd come over.

"Let me take your jacket then follow the enthusiastic kid for cookies."

Zack reached over and brushed his lips against hers. His were cool. The kiss was too brief, but still caused Susan to catch her breath. Her gaze dropped to his jacket. When he took it off, she hung it up, feeling the warmth from his body.

"Here you go," Danny said, coming out of the kitchen holding a plate of cookies. It tipped dangerously.

"Hey, thanks, buddy." Zack moved swiftly to get the plate from the little boy before all the cookies landed on the floor.

"These look great. You made them?" he asked Danny.

The child smiled widely and nodded his head. "Mommy said I could help."

"Good for mommy. How are they?" Zack took one and bit into it. "Delicious!" he declared turning to look at Susan.

Susan walked past him, catching a hint of his scent—aftershave and Zack. It kicked up her pulse rate. She was glad she'd brushed her hair, put on fresh lipstick and made sure all traces of flour were gone from her dark sweater.

"Danny loves to make cookies so any rainy day, that's often a project," she said, feeling suddenly shy and as awkward as a schoolgirl. "Want some milk or coffee to go with that?"

"Do you have hot chocolate?"

"Yes. That would be good for all of us on such a day," she said, heading for the kitchen. Making the hot chocolate would give her something to do until her nerves calmed down.

Zack followed her and put the plate of cookies on the counter.

Danny rushed in and looked around. "Aren't you going to eat the cookies?" he asked.

"I had one. I'll have another when your mom has the hot chocolate ready."

"I like marshmallows in mine," Danny said. In a moment, bored, he left.

Zack leaned against the doorjamb and watched as Susan prepared their hot drinks.

"If I didn't have to act like an adult," Zack began, "I'd gobble up all those cookies. But I had better be a good example to an impressionable kid."

She laughed. "Good idea. How was your walk over?"

"Cold. I think the temperature dropped twenty degrees. But it felt good."

"I'm ready for summer. It was cold all winter long. I think this is ready. Want to call Danny for me?"

"I'll go get him," Zack said.

Zack returned a moment later, carrying a laughing Danny.

"Found him."

"We'll sit at the table. It's less chancy for him spilling things," she said, pointing to the small round table with three chairs that served as her dining area. Sometimes Edith shared a meal with them, so Susan had three chairs. This would be the first guest she'd had in the apartment except for Edith.

"We went to see Edith," Danny said. "She's sick."

"Did you take her cookies?"

"Yes! We make the bestest cookies," Danny said.

"She has the flu…not too interested in cookies," Susan added.

Zack looked at Susan. "Will she be able to watch this young man in the morning?"

"No. She didn't look so good when we saw her earlier. I've been calling around to find someone."

"Any luck?"

"Two of my backup women already have plans. The third is also sick. Apparently the flu is going around."

"Don't you get sick," Zack said.

"Exactly what Danny said," she replied. "I'll do my best not to. But Edith has been such a help to me, I need to return the favor and help her out when she's sick. She doesn't have anyone else. I thought I'd go down before supper to make sure she doesn't need anything more today."

"Why don't you leave Danny here when you check on her? No sense exposing him to germs if you don't have to."

"Thanks," she said, "He's been there, but stayed in the living room. I feel really badly for her—having no one to take care of her when she's sick."

"Who takes care of you when you're sick?" he asked, taking another cookie.

"No one. She'd help, I'm sure. Fortunately, I'm rarely sick."

"I want to get down. I'm finished," Danny said.

"I should find a way to burn off some of that energy," she said, helping Danny to the floor, pushing his empty cup away from the edge of the table.

"If it weren't so late, we could take him to a

museum or someplace indoors and let him run around."

"But it is late and it's started raining again. I wish it would rain at night and leave the daylight for kids to play outside."

"Does this mean the preschool is leaking again?" he asked, turning to look out the window.

"I hope not. The roof was repaired. It's the water damage from the previous leak that needs fixing."

They finished their chocolate and then moved into the living room. Susan asked him to stay for dinner and Zack quickly accepted. He explained he'd never turn down a home-cooked meal.

They talked in between playing with Danny and finally settling in to watch a Disney movie.

When Susan went in to prepare dinner, Zack stayed in the main part of the apartment to entertain Danny.

She dashed down just before eating to check on Edith. Satisfied the older woman was holding her own, she returned and dished up dinner for the three of them.

Sitting at the table she was reminded of meals with Tom. Danny had been too little to eat his meals at the table; he'd still been in a high chair. Looking up once she was startled to see Zack's dark hair and eyes when she expected to see Tom's light brown.

By the time dinner was over, Danny was growing sleepy.

"What did you do to my son?" she asked when he yawned again at the table.

"We had races. I remember one foster mother having all the kids race around the yard to wear us out. He loved it."

"You ran around with him?"

"No, I timed him with my watch. And he got faster and faster, didn't you, Dano?" Zack said.

"Yes, I can run fast as a superhero," he said. "Want to see?" Without waiting for Susan's answer, he got off the chair and raced down the hall. A moment later she could hear his footsteps as he ran back.

"Very good. And what a great idea, as long as he doesn't drive the downstairs neighbors crazy."

Zack and Danny helped clear the table and then Zack stayed in the kitchen with Susan while she quickly did the dishes. It was cozy, the rain on the window, the companionship of the two of them while she washed and set the dishes in the drainer.

She glanced over at Zack. He was watching her as if he'd never seen a woman washing dishes before.

"What?" she asked.

"Soaking in the atmosphere," he said slowly.

"Dishwashing?"

"Different from the desert. And from having a real kitchen. The room where I'm staying doesn't have much except a small refrigerator. I order in when not invited for a home-cooked meal."

"Every night?"

"And lunch, too. Breakfast I usually catch at the local coffeehouse."

"What do you do when on the job site? Surely they don't have restaurants on every corner over there," she asked.

"We usually have a mess tent. No point in fifty men each cooking for themselves if the company can have a cook to prepare meals for everyone. Keeps morale high and men focused on the work they were hired for."

"So that's kind of home-cooked," she said, wiping down the counters and turning to face him. He looked tired. She forgot sometimes he was still recovering from being hit by a land mine. Had Danny worn him out?

"Don't confuse mess food with home-cooked. Yours is the best."

Delighting in his compliment, she smiled. "You're easy to please," she said. She draped the dishrag over the sink edge and wiped her hands on the towel. Hanging it on the rack, she turned. Zack was just inches away.

"I meant it, Susan," he said, his voice low and sexy.

He reached out to put his hands on her shoulders, pulling her closer. His mouth covered hers and Susan let out a soft sigh as the magic of his kiss took over.

She kissed him back, wanting a closer contact. Stepping closer, she put her arms around his neck and was delighted to have him encircle her with his arms and pull her in for full body contact.

It was the most exciting kiss she'd ever had. Every cell in her body tingled with anticipation. Her mouth grew greedy, moving against his, relishing every press of lips, every sweep of his tongue. His hands splayed on her back, pressing her into him. She could feel the weight of them, wondering what they'd feel like on her bare skin.

Time had no meaning as the kiss continued. Susan could have stayed in Zack's arms forever.

He moved from her mouth to kiss her cheek, along her jawline, down her throat.

Susan flung her head back, eyes still closed as she relished every tantalizing touch of his mouth against her skin. When he kissed the rapid pulse point at the base of the throat, she clung, shivering in pleasure.

"Mommy, why is Zack biting your neck?" Danny asked.

The moment shattered. Susan pulled back so fast she almost lost her balance. Zack's hand on her arm steadied her.

"I wasn't biting your mother, I was kissing her," Zack said.

Susan couldn't utter a sound. How could she have forgotten her son? What was she doing kissing a man she hardly knew? This was so wrong.

"Why?" Danny asked.

"I like her. When people like each other, sometimes they kiss each other," Zack said, stooping down to be at Danny's eye level.

"Know how your mommy kisses you good-night when you go to bed?"

Danny nodded.

"That's because she loves you and wants to kiss you to sleep at night."

Danny looked at Susan, a frown on his face. "But she doesn't kiss me so long."

"Ah, that's a special kind of kiss between a man and a woman. When you are all grown up, you'll understand."

"You need to take a quick bath, get in jammies and get to bed," Susan said. She reached out for Danny's hand, afraid to look at Zack. No telling what he thought of her wanton display. She wasn't sure what to make of it herself.

"Want help?" he asked.

"No," she said quickly. Taking a quick breath she tried to smile. "We'll just be a few minutes." She wished he'd offer to leave, but he merely nodded and slid his hands into the side pockets of his slacks.

"I'll wait, then."

"Want to give me a bath?" Danny asked hopefully.

"Not tonight," Susan responded before Zack could. She needed a few moments away from him!

Twenty minutes later, Danny was in pajamas and ran to the living room to bid Zack good-night.

"Mommy's going to read my story tonight. Maybe you can another night," he said gravely.

"I look forward to it," Zack said, reaching down to give him a quick hug.

Susan had her emotions under control by the time she returned to the living room a short time later.

"Danny asleep?" Zack asked, rising as she entered.

"Yes." She smiled and paused for a moment, then deliberately sat on the sofa. Zack sat beside her.

"I've been thinking," he began.

She almost held her breath. Had he been thinking the same thing she had been? That there was something special between them? She wasn't sure if she wanted to discuss it, but there was no denying it was there.

"If you can't find another sitter, I could watch Danny for you when he's not in preschool."

"I couldn't ask you to do that," she said. So much for her intuition of what he wanted to talk about.

"I have ample time. And I'm going a bit cabin crazy with this enforced inactivity. Unless you don't think I can handle him. Or you don't trust me."

Susan looked at him in surprise.

"It's not that. You're recuperating. You need rest. Not to be running after a four-year-old all day."

"People atrophy if they do nothing. I'm used to working all day almost every day. This sitting around is getting to me."

"You don't think he'll wear you out?"

Zack shook his head. "If I get too tired, I'll nap when he does. But how hard can it be to watch a four-year-old?"

Susan grinned. "Harder than I expect you believe it'll be." She thought about it another moment and then nodded slowly. "You are a lifesaver. I thought I was going to have to take time off from work to watch him. No one seems available tomorrow. I'll take you up on your offer only if you promise to call me if things get out of hand."

"They won't," he said confidently.

Susan hoped he was correct. One of the hardest parts of being a parent was finding child care. Edith had been a lifesaver. The arrangement had worked perfectly for the two of them. But when she was ill, it was hard to get someone on such short notice.

Zack slid a bit closer, put his arm across the back of the sofa and looked at her. His fingers brushed against her hair. Susan resisted the urge to bolt from the room. She leaned back slightly and tried to relax, which was impossible with her heart racing like it was.

"It's supposed to stop raining tonight. Would the park be too wet for him to play tomorrow?" Zack asked, his caressing fingers causing her great difficulty in thinking straight.

"I'll give you a towel to wipe down the slide if you're the first ones there. After a couple of kids have been on them, they're dry. Are you sure?"

"About what?" he asked, looking into her eyes.

Susan felt her heart rate increase. "About watching Danny."

"Yes."

"Thanks."

"If you keep looking at me like that, I'm going to forget there's a little boy asleep down the hall and a sick woman you need to check and do something that might be construed as moving too fast," he said in his low voice.

Susan reached out to touch his cheek, moving her fingers to his lips. Zack kissed them, sending a shock of awareness through her.

He took her hand and placed a kiss in the palm, closing her fingers over. "Go check on Mrs. Jordan. I'm going home soon. I'll stay here until then."

"About moving too fast?"

"Yes?"

"I don't know if I'm even ready to move on. I loved Tom very much."

"Let's just see what happens. Tell me if I'm pushing too hard," he replied, kissing her fingers.

"I like that," she said softly.

"I do, too," he said, kissing her again.

"I'd better check on Mrs. J and then let you go home. Thanks for the offer. I really appreciate it."

"It'll be my pleasure."

* * *

When Susan left, Zack rose and went to see his son again. Danny was asleep, looking angelic. Tomorrow Zack would be able to spend the entire day with him. He smiled, remembering some of the antics and comments the child had made that afternoon. Were all children as endearing or was there a special bond because of their blood ties? He didn't know or care. He loved this child. Tomorrow they'd build on the memories they were making.

He walked back to the living room, standing by the window to watch the rain. It had been challenging to think up activities this afternoon to entertain without any prior experience.

The visit to the park had been easier. Of course he'd let Susan take the lead and she knew more about Danny's likes and activities. Maybe he could get her to show him the pictures of his son from infancy. Zack yearned to learn all he could about Danny.

Zack turned back to look at the room—and all the pictures. Thomas Johnson, obviously, he thought, lifting one of the frames and studying the man who had adopted his son. He looked solid, someone to depend upon. Another showed Tom and Susan at the beach, laughing in the sun. There were several with Tom holding a baby and then a toddler as Danny grew. According to the detective, Danny had been two when Thomas Johnson had been killed by that hit and run drunken driver. The man had been apprehended later and charged with manslaughter. Did that help at all with Susan's loss?

He doubted it. She had that constant hint of sadness in her eyes.

Putting the picture down, he surveyed the rest of the room as he went to sit on the chair near the sofa. It was casually decorated, lots of pictures and books. The television sat unobtrusively in one corner. It was a good room for a little boy.

When he heard the key in the door, he turned.

"She's doing about the same and promised to call her doctor in the morning. I told her Danny was taken care of and that seemed to take a load off her mind."

"Does she need someone to care for her?" he asked.

"I heated some more soup for her and made some toast. She said that was all she wanted. I made sure she was drinking plenty of fluids. Other than that, I think she wants to be left alone."

"I do when I'm sick."

"Most guys do. I remember Tom—" She stopped abruptly. "Never mind. I hope I don't catch it from her. There's nothing worse than being incapacitated with a four-year-old running around."

"What time should I be here in the morning?" he asked, rising.

"I usually leave around 8:30. Want to come a bit earlier to make sure the transition goes smoothly?

It'll be something extraordinary for Danny. I'm sure he'll be delighted, but just to make sure there are no problems."

Zack nodded. He wanted to stay, to talk more to Susan, but it was already after nine and she had to work tomorrow.

"See you then," he said, crossing the room. "Walk me to the door?"

It was only about ten steps, but he wanted to kiss her good-night. She went with him and looked up expectantly when they reached the door.

"I enjoyed dinner," he said, leaning down to kiss her. He'd only wanted to brush her lips with his, but once they touched, he felt desire rise. He wanted more. Susan was willing and opened her mouth at the first hint from him.

Wrapping her in his arms, he kissed her as he had in the kitchen. Ending the kiss too soon, he rested his forehead against hers. "Thanks again for dinner," he said.

"Thanks for watching my son," she replied, her eyes luminescent.

Zack rode the elevator down to the lobby. He wasn't sure he was going about this the right way. He was beginning to want Susan in a totally different way. And to feel guilty about not telling her about his relationship to Danny. It was becoming complex when all he'd started out to do was catch a glimpse of his son. Now he knew him, knew he was happy and thriving.

Susan had been unexpected—as were the growing emotions and attachment he was feeling for her. How would she take learning he was Danny's biological father? Would she send him packing? Become distant but allow him to continue visiting with them?

Or was she beginning to feel something more for him as he was for her? Could it lead to marriage? Or would telling her end everything?

Could they make a family? It would be the perfect solution. Only—she'd said she wasn't sure she was ready to move on. The bond between her and Tom apparently had not been broken when he died. As evidenced by all the photos all over the flat and her constant references to him. To see how far they could explore this relationship, she needed to move on.

What could he do to help? He didn't want to feel second best. If their relationship developed, would she ever care for him as much as for her first husband? Would he end up accepting whatever she gave just to stay near?

CHAPTER SIX

BY TUESDAY, Zack knew he loved being a dad. He and Danny had spent Monday going to the park in the morning. He fixed them both peanut butter and jelly sandwiches for lunch and read him a story before his nap. That afternoon they played at the park again. The more time they spent together, the more Zack knew he was doing the right thing in connecting with his son. What would it be like to be with him until he grew up? To have a part in molding him to manhood?

He looked forward to the evening when Susan returned home. Together they'd prepared dinner. The meals proved lively. Danny hopped from one topic to another. Laughter was common. Zack liked watching Susan when she talked. Her eyes didn't hold as much sadness as he'd once seen. Her laughter was light and delightful. He did his best to keep it going.

And after Danny was in bed, the two adults had a time to talk. Edith was on the mend. She told

Susan she'd be ready to watch Danny again in a day or two. Which meant only a couple of more days alone with his son. His scheduled trip to the U.N. to see where Susan worked was postponed while he watched Danny. But he'd make sure to reschedule when things were back to normal. He wanted to see her in her work space, see who she worked with, what her friends were like.

He had the Wednesday meeting at the school to attend, which would give him more insight into her life. Once he had worried he couldn't fit in with her and Danny, but now he was willing to try.

Tuesday while Danny napped, Zack attempted to read. But his gaze was drawn again and again to the many photographs of Tom Johnson that were scattered around the living room. He had also noted an enlargement of one by Danny's bed. Were they there for Danny's sake, or Susan's? Zack wasn't sure.

He was drawn to Susan and she seemed receptive to his kisses. Yet last weekend she had clearly stated she wasn't ready to move on. It was obvious from the pictures that the three of them had been a very happy family. Wistfully, Zack wondered if he'd ever find that kind of happiness.

It was too soon to suggest to Susan that she consider marrying him. He'd only known her a couple of weeks. Yet the rightness wouldn't go away. It all depended upon Susan.

* * *

Susan unlocked the door, excited to see the two men in her life these days. Zack had been a huge help these two days. Danny had adored having Zack watch him. That morning he'd gone to preschool and Zack had called to check in with her in the afternoon and told her he'd felt like an elephant in a china shop, but had persevered, running the gauntlet of mothers. She remembered laughing at his recount.

The best time of the day was after she returned home. Being with Zack reminded her of the evenings she and Tom had shared—preparing the meal, talking about their days. But the aching sense of loss she had experienced for the last two years was missing. Being with Zack brought out the best of being a couple with none of the crushing reminders of her dead husband.

"Mommy!" Danny raced down the hall to greet her, flinging his arms around her legs as high as he could reach.

"Hey, sweet thing, how are you?" Susan picked him up to hug, her eyes going to the tall man following him at a more discreet pace.

"Zack and me went to the park."

"I know, he told me he was taking you there." Sharing the look with Zack felt right. When he was close enough, he leaned in and kissed her, then looked at Danny, still in his mother's arms.

"Did you kiss Mommy?" Zack asked.

Danny kissed her then smiled at Zack. He struggled to get down, then ran back toward his room. "I got a ball," he said.

Susan put her purse on the small table and took off her light jacket. "You bought him another toy? Honestly, where is he going to put them all?"

"Hey, a ball, a battery powered car and a kite are hardly going to force you to live elsewhere. Besides, I have as much fun with them as he does."

"I know, two boys at heart."

He pulled her into his arms and gave her a real kiss. "I may be a boy at heart, but around you, I feel all man," he said a moment later.

Danny returned with his ball before Susan could respond. She admired the new ball that was almost as large as Danny. Then said, "I need to change clothes, then who wants to help me with dinner?"

"Me and Zack! Me and Zack!" Danny shouted.

Susan laughed. But as she walked toward her room she began to wonder how her son was going to react when his time with Zack would be curtailed. Or what would happen in a couple of months when Zack moved on? Would he keep in touch? She hoped so. She couldn't imagine never seeing him again.

Once in casual clothes, she hurried out to the kitchen to start dinner.

When Danny had been put to bed and it was just the two of them, Susan became quiet. She was getting too used to this arrangement. Danny wasn't the only one who was going to miss Zack when he wasn't around.

"How about showing me those pictures of Danny when he was younger," Zack suggested when she walked into the living room.

"A great idea to a mother, but you'll be bored after a while."

"I doubt it," he said. He had wanted to see the early pictures for days. He yearned to know all he could about Danny, from if he'd been a fussy baby to when he took his first steps. Surely Susan would like sharing that.

She went to the bookcase and pulled out two bulging albums and carried them to the sofa.

Opening the first, she caught her breath as the memory hit. It showed her holding a bundled up Danny in front of the building where they all used to live. She remembered Tom had wanted to have a picture of Danny's first home in case they moved later. Neither suspected Susan and Danny would be moving without Tom.

"He's about a week old here," she said, pointing to the picture. Slowly she gave a brief comment on each picture as they leafed through the album. To Zack's delight, she noted memorial events. Here was the photo of Danny's first tooth. Looked like a lot of gum to Zack, but Susan assured him that tiny speck on the lower gum was a tooth that had just broken through.

She had several of him standing, looking astonished. "Here's when he took his first step. I wish I had a movie camera. These are just still shots." The little boy had been by the sofa, moving toward the camera. There were four photos shot rapidly showing the steps and the crash landing on his diapered bottom.

There were also locks of hair and handprints and footprints from his one-month checkup, notations of his height and weight at each doctor's visit.

Zack studied each photograph, asking her questions through all the pictures. Slowly they moved through almost four years worth of photos in the two albums. There was a gap when Danny first turned two—when Tom had died. It had been weeks before Susan had felt up to taking pictures and able to do so without tears blurring her vision.

The memories were bittersweet, but she went through both albums with Zack. It was her life with Danny recorded, even though Tom was now gone. She was glad she had all the pictures she did.

"My goodness, it's after ten. You weren't bored, were you?" she asked when she closed the second book.

"Not at all. You've done a good job, raising him. It can't be easy as a solo parent. I know he's run me ragged these two days."

She put the book on the coffee table and leaned back against the cushions. "Sometimes I wonder how I can do it, other times I wouldn't change a thing. He's the light of my life."

"Did you ever want more children?"

"Tom and I talked about having three, but it wasn't to be. How about you? How many kids do you want?"

"I never planned on getting married. That might change, however." Zack looked at her. "Would you go out with me Saturday night—to dinner. Maybe dancing if I can find a place. Just you and me."

Susan felt her heart rate increase. This would be a date. No camouflaging it with a little boy as a buffer. No confusing the issue by saying they were just going on a picnic as new acquaintances or bumping into each other at the park. An honest-to-goodness date.

"Yes, I'd like to," she replied. Then a wave of panic doused her. What was she thinking? She glanced at the nearest picture of Tom.

"I hate that," Zack said.

She looked at him. "What?"

"You look at his picture all the time. As if asking permission, or forgiveness for moving on. How long are you going to depend on a dead man? How long are you going to live in the past? He sounds like he was a wonderful person who loved you a lot. But he's gone, never to come back. I wish you would acknowledge that and move on."

Susan felt as if he'd slapped her.

"I don't depend on a dead man as you so crudely put it. He was my husband. I loved him dearly. I miss him." She jumped up and crossed to the window, staring out to the darkness. How dare Zack say she was stuck in the past.

"I know that makes you angry. But look at it from my point of view. Every time I kiss you I feel he's right there in the middle of us. I want to treat you like a woman, yet I feel we have a chaperone in our midst. I know he was a good man. A loving husband and father. But he's gone and you are not. You need to move on. Make a new life for yourself, not be put on hold."

"I know that. He was my husband. Am I supposed to forget he existed? I have made a new life. I have a job, a new apartment. I'm doing the best I can. Maybe if you'd ever been deeply in love and lost, you'd understand. But you seem too afraid to form attachments. Moving around like you do makes it convenient to keep everyone at a distance. Well, I'm coping the best I can."

"It's been two years. Surely you've made some closure. Come to terms with it."

"I have," she said with dignity. Then frowned. "I think."

He rose and moved to stand beside her, not touching, but close enough to feel the warmth from her body, to smell the sweet scent she wore.

"I'm not sure how close we'll ever become if Tom Johnson is in the middle."

"He's not." Susan realized suddenly it was taking a lot of energy to keep from looking at his picture at this moment. Was she still depending on Tom?

She really enjoyed being with Zack. She looked forward to seeing him, hearing about his day with Danny, learning about his life.

"No one can measure up to him. Especially now that he's gone forever. No man can compete," Zack said.

"And are you trying to compete?"

He hesitated a moment then slowly nodded. "Maybe."

That surprised her. Was he really courting her? Panic flared. She wasn't ready to be more than friends.

"I'd like to think we are friends," she said slowly.

"I think I'm jealous," he admitted.

"Of a dead man?"

"It's hard to compete with a ghost," Zack said wryly.

"You don't have to compete with anyone." She turned, stepped closer, erasing the distance between them. "I think you are very special and I want to go out—just the two of us. As long as I can get a baby-sitter. I don't know if Edith will be up to it by Saturday."

"Then we go if you can get a sitter," he said. "I'll head for home now. I'll be here again in the morning."

He stepped around her and left.

Susan spun around, astonished he hadn't kissed her good-night. Glaring at the door for a moment, she shifted her gaze to Tom's closest picture. She did look at them all the time. They kept her connected. But Zack was right, Tom was dead. Her mother had said clinging to the past wouldn't bring him back. Tears filled her eyes. Her first love was gone forever. For the millionth time she wished she could turn back the clock. Hold on to what they had. She yearned for his touch, his humor, his love. It had vanished two years ago, never to be again.

Walking over, she picked up her favorite picture and gazed into the dear face she'd never see again. She could hear the echo of his voice, his laugh. She could see the love in his eyes.

"I loved you," she murmured. "It about killed me when you went. If I hadn't had Danny, I don't know how I could have coped. He's such a great kid. You would have enjoyed watching him grow up, and would have taught him so much."

She thought about it for a long moment, then sighed softly.

"Actually, Zack is teaching him things. How to be responsible. How to share. And a bit about families—even though he didn't have one of his own."

She hugged the frame against her chest—it was cold and hard.

With a deep sigh, she went slowly around the room and collected the pictures of Tom, reliving all the memories that flooded when she viewed each one. He would forever be part of her life. But it was time to move on. Maybe to another chapter that could be just as happy.

When she had all the photographs in her arms, she went to the bedroom and placed them in the bottom drawer of the dresser that had been Tom's. She'd let the one stay in Danny's room. And the one by her bed. A child should remember his father. And she wanted to see his dear face a few more mornings when she first woke.

Feeling nostalgic and a bit melancholy, she went to bed. Stretching out her hand, she felt the empty space beside her. Never to be filled, she'd once thought. Now she wondered if Zack would like to pursue their relationship all the way to making love. Closing her eyes, she could almost imagine his strong body pulling her close, his deep voice speaking to her in the night. The joy they'd share making love and sleeping together. Waking up together.

Where once she never expected to share a bed with another, now she wondered if she could imagine not eventually sharing her bed with Zack.

Rolling on her side, she remembered Zack's kisses, his hands caressing her. If things kept on the way they were going, would they fall for each other? Or was she just someone to fill the time while he was on leave? She hoped not. Zack Morgan was a very special man. She closed her eyes. No one could predict the future. But she might just open herself up to whatever came—embracing every new experience.

Wednesday Zack showed up just as Susan was beginning to think he wasn't coming. She had to leave immediately. He had timed it that way, she suspected. But there wasn't enough time to challenge him on the issue. At least he had arrived and she could get to work.

"I'll be home in time to cook a quick dinner so we can leave for the school," she said as she was walking out the door. She looked back. "You are still going?"

"I said I would," he replied, his attention already on Danny.

The day seemed interminable to Susan. She couldn't concentrate on her translations for wondering what Zack and Danny were doing. She hoped he wouldn't regret offering his help. Edith had told her last night when she went to check on her that she felt up to watching Danny for the evening. It would only be for an hour or two and he'd be going to bed at eight.

Torn between wanting to see Zack again, and dreading the confrontation for the churning emotions that filled her, Susan wasn't sure how she felt as she caught the subway for home. Walking in the door just before six, she could smell something delicious cooking.

"I'm home," she called out.

Danny came running from the kitchen. "Zack made dinner," he said, his face full of wonder.

Zack appeared in the doorway, looking as unlike a cook as anyone she'd ever seen. His broad shoulders almost filled the doorway. His attire would be suited to a work site—jeans and a chambray shirt, unbuttoned at the throat with the sleeves rolled up. He looked rugged and handsome. She caught her breath and then smiled.

"What a treat," she said.

"Just burgers and fries," he said.

She didn't correct him. If he thought she meant the food, that was fine by her.

"I'll change and be right out."

"Be ready in about ten. I thought I timed it about right," he said with satisfaction. His gaze moved over her and his eyes seemed to light up.

Feeling flustered, Susan spun around and almost ran to her bedroom. She changed quickly, seeking Tom's photograph. "It is a habit. I hope you won't mind if I break it. If I can," she murmured. Feeling like a soldier going off to war with no armor, she bravely went to have dinner with the most exciting man she'd known.

When they walked over to the school, he took her hand. "I see you put away Tom's pictures."

"Yes." She couldn't say any more. She felt as if she ripped off a Band-Aid. But it was healthy. She would never forget him. Now was time to explore new options and opportunities.

He didn't say anything, either, but the clasp of his hand warmed her.

Promptly at seven the meeting began. Susan had felt extremely self-conscious walking into the school's largest room with Zack at her side. He looked completely out of his element dwarfing the small furniture more suitable to preschoolers than the men and women who had assembled.

The meeting went well, with all parents volunteering for some tasks. There was not a lot of money in the entire group, Susan thought, but they were all parents interested in providing the best for their children.

When Zack volunteered to work on the drywall in two classrooms and the playground upgrade, heads swiveled and questions were whispered as no one recognized him. "I'm here for Danny Johnson," he said.

Speculative glances then moved to Susan from the parents who knew her. She felt awkward. Still, she was glad Danny had someone who could be of more help than she would be. She signed up for painting, both indoors and out. She hoped the weather would cooperate. The first work weekend was in three days. They were scheduled out for a month, then a reassessment would be made to determine how much more work still needed to be done.

"I know most of us have busy lives and can hardly afford the school fees. But working together, we'll pass the city's inspection and keep the school open," the headmistress said at the conclusion of the meeting.

"Thanks again," Susan said to Zack as they rose in preparation to leave. "It's probably minuscule compared to what you normally do."

"It is, but I'll have more direct interaction than I normally do. I'm the boss on the sites. Here I'll get to swing a hammer."

"Oh, fun," she murmured.

"I want to talk to the headmistress. If she hasn't already ordered the supplies, I might be able to help."

They moved toward Mrs. Harper, waiting while two other parents chatted with her for a few minutes. Then it was their turn.

"I'm Zack Morgan."

"I remember seeing you when we had that scare when Danny ran off. So nice of you to volunteer to help us," she said extending her hand and then smiling at Susan.

"If you don't already have your supplies, I might be able to get them at a lower cost." He quickly explained what company he worked for. "One thing the company is always looking for is community projects it can support. I think I can call one of the men in the local office and get supplies at a deep discount."

"Oh, that would be so helpful. We are really stretched on this. We really can't afford these repairs, but if we don't do them, we'll be closed down. I can't let that happen. The hardware store a few blocks away was giving us a ten percent discount. I thought it was the best I could do."

"I'm sure my company will beat that. I'll make some calls in the morning and then let you know."

She smiled and nodded, turning to Susan. "I'm so grateful for your help and your friend's."

"He's in construction, I bet he knows every trick of the trade," she said.

Mrs. Harper's eyes widened. "Oh, perfect. Can you handle the building inspector when he comes? I always feel like he's talking another language."

"Sure," Zack said.

She reached out to shake his hand again. "I can't thank you enough," she said smiling broadly.

On the walk back to Susan's apartment, she glanced at him. He looked as if he were deep in thought.

"Can you really get some bargain rates?" she asked.

He nodded. "Our company is big on supporting local communities, whether here or on location. It builds goodwill."

"This will build a heap of goodwill. As you can imagine, this place runs on a shoestring. Why are you taking such an interest?"

"Told you—"

"There's more to this than you're bored. You could find other things to occupy your time. You hardly know us, why would you do this?"

"It's a good project. And I know you and Danny. Why wouldn't I want to help? It's not much."

"It's a lot."

"Only because no one else there has a construction background. This is sort of like baking cookies for me," Zack said.

Susan laughed aloud. "Baking cookies?"

"Something you do almost without thinking, right?"

She nodded.

"This is nothing compared to building a bridge. Repair a few walls, refurbish some playground equipment. You and the other women will be doing the painting. This is a walk in the park." He reached out and caught her hand in his. "Besides, I get to spend more time with you."

Saturday was bright and clear. Edith had insisted she was well enough to watch Danny while Zack and Susan worked at the school—and that evening when the two of them were going out.

Susan was excited about the date. She had her whole day planned in her mind, including dashing home from the school to shower and change in time for dinner.

When her mother called, she almost blurted it out, but she wasn't up to a thousand questions, which her mother would have had. Instead she kept the conversation short, telling her mother she had to leave soon for the school project. The day started at nine and Mrs. Harper had urged parents to stay until five. Pizza was being ordered in for lunch.

Susan knew several of the mothers of the children in Danny's class. They greeted one another and began the tasks as assigned. Zack gathered tools that had been provided and moved to another room. Two men from his company had also shown up to help. They greeted each other and suddenly Susan felt left out. She watched as they caught up on their lives and observed Zack in his element. All three men were tall, rugged individuals. Competent and assured in their success, but not overblown or arrogant, they quickly set to work and before the morning was finished, it was clear the school had been lucky to get these volunteers. Work procedures were set out and followed. The genial air of camaraderie made it a festive atmosphere.

"Who's your friend," Betsy Singleton asked Susan as they began moving furnishings and scrubbing the stained portion on a wall deemed safe enough to repaint and not repair.

"Zack Morgan. He's only here temporarily," Susan said.

"Too bad. He's a hunk. Bet Danny loves being around him."

Susan nodded. "He does."

"I heard about Danny's running away the other day. That must have been scary."

Susan agreed. "But he seems to have stopped doing that." In the days since they'd met Zack, Danny hadn't run after a stranger once. For that she was grateful, but wondered what he would do when Zack left. She hoped her little boy wouldn't be heartbroken again.

The morning sped by. Susan was glad for the lunch break. Her shoulders hurt from pushing a paint roller. Since the day was nice, the pizza was served in the playground with a long table set up holding the food and beverages.

Zack joined her once they both picked up their plates. They sat on one of the benches lining the playground. Betsy and her husband shared the bench.

"Brad Singleton," he introduced himself to Zack and Susan. She introduced them both and settled in to eat.

"You really know what you're doing," Brad said to Zack. "I think we'd all be floundering around without you and your buddies helping."

"This is a straight forward project," Zack said. He took a bite of pizza, chewed it and then took a long swallow of the soft drink he'd chosen. "I'm surprised at how many parents turned out. Looks like most of them, would you say?"

Brad glanced around. "At least. And there are two teenagers from our church helping out. Plus your two friends. We might get it all fixed up before the time frame Mrs. Harper set."

"Could. Once some of the men are shown what to do, they manage fine," Zack said.

"Not something we're all used to. You're in construction, I think I heard someone say."

Zack nodded, glancing at Susan. She smiled at him.

"Glad to have someone aboard who knows what to do."

"Apparently Mrs. Harper thinks so," Susan added. "She's asked Zack to be the contact guy for the building inspector."

"Hey, that's cool. I'm sure you know what to do to get us passed first time. We can't afford a different preschool for Bethany. I'd hate for her to lose this chance at getting a jump on schooling."

The discussion veered to talking about the children. Susan was amused to find Zack listening for all he was worth. He didn't contribute much on that topic, but a couple of times agreed when he remembered something Danny had said or done.

Lunch went too fast.

The afternoon turned out better as everyone got into a rhythm. The festive atmosphere continued as everyone knew they were pulling together for their children and the sake of the school.

Promptly at four forty-five, Mrs. Harper began

her rounds advising people to finish up so they could leave at five. "Tomorrow we'll start at one to give everyone a chance to sleep in and also go to church. I'm amazed at all that's been done today." She came over to Susan. "And it's all thanks to your friend Zack. He's been a marvel. He works twice as fast as the others and the work is impeccable. And he got all the supplies and tools donated. I can't tell you what that means. It's amazing. We won't be in the red at the end of the school term. And we'll have one of the nicest preschools—and safest—in this area. And so I told him!"

Susan felt a warm glow of pride for Zack's sake. He was volunteering when he should be recuperating. He chose to spend his Saturday helping out a school where he had no one attending. Only the son of a new friend.

Maybe more than a friend?

At five Zack wandered into the classroom, examining the painting. "Did good, ladies," he said with a smile. The other women beamed at his compliment. Susan smiled as well. Forgotten was her tiredness. She was glad she could help.

"Ready to go?" he asked her.

"Yes."

"Not too tired to go out to dinner, are you?" he asked as they began walking toward her apartment.

"No. Are you?"

"I feel fine. Better than fine. Might be the best thing I've done for a while."

"Good."

He stopped outside her apartment building. "I'll go clean up and be back here at seven."

"Okay. See you then." She walked briskly to the elevator and only when the doors closed behind her did she sag against the wall. She was so tired she could scarcely keep her eyes open. But she would not admit that to anyone. She wanted to go out with Zack tonight.

Danny and Edith greeted her. Edith was back to normal and had prepared a small dinner for her and Danny. She asked after the school renovations.

"You went to my school?" Danny asked.

"Yes, Zack and I worked on getting it fixed up. It's going to look terrific before you know it. And it will pass all the inspections the city requires. Zack worked harder than anyone," she told him.

"I want to go with Zack," Danny said.

"On Tuesday when you go to school, you ask the teacher to show you where Zack worked, okay?"

"'Kay."

As Susan prepared for her date, she felt butterflies in her stomach. She had been on two other dates since Tom had died, both a bust in her opinion. The first man was nice enough, but they had so little to talk about. The second had not been especially fond of children and had at one point during the evening asked if she would not talk about her son so much. That had been an instant turnoff.

After those experiences, she'd declined all other invitations to dinner. She was happier with Danny than with men she scarcely knew.

Zack was different. For one thing, he really liked her son. For another, he enticed her like no other. His kisses drove her crazy. And his calm approach to life was like a balm. She worried all the time that she alone wouldn't be able to raise Danny, yet around Zack she felt confident. He had told her more than once she was doing a good job.

The dress she put on was new. Was it sexy enough to get Zack to sit up and take notice? She pictured him with eyes for only her. She made a face at her fantasy and brushed her hair. Putting on her lipstick, she was ready. Taking a deep breath, she tried to quell her nerves. For heaven's sake, she and Zack had spent hours together over the last couple of weeks. This was merely a time for adults, no Danny around. Not so different.

And she vowed she would not talk about her son all night. Though what they would talk about other than Danny was beyond her at the moment. If not for Danny, they never would have met.

Edith was talking with Danny, and Susan could hear the soft murmur of her voice. He was miffed he wasn't included in tonight's outing. While sympathetic, Susan nevertheless had told him that there were some things he didn't get and he needed to learn that young. Edith was reinforcing the sentiment.

She heard the knock at the door as she stepped out of her bedroom. And Danny's "I'll get it!"

She started to protest, but it would do little good.

When she could see the door, she was surprised to find Zack down at Danny's level talking to him. The little boy was nodding, looking solemn.

Zack stood when he saw Susan and smiled. Her heart fluttered. He looked devastatingly handsome in the dark suit and white shirt. His tie was silver and blue. She had never seen him in a suit before. He was dynamite. Every woman who saw him tonight would envy her. Susan smiled. It felt good.

"I'm ready," she said. "What are you up to, Danny?" she asked.

"I'm not going to answer the door without you telling me," he said, his lower lip sticking out suspiciously like a pout.

"That's very good." She looked at Zack with a question in her eyes.

"I told Danny he needs to develop responsibility so he'll be a fine man when he grows up. One way is to mind his mommy when you tell him not to do something."

"Ah." She looked at her son. He seemed resigned. "That is very good advice."

Danny turned and ran back to the living room. He

climbed up on the sofa beside Edith and looked at the cartoon movies they'd been watching.

"I'm leaving now." Susan went to kiss Danny goodbye and exchange last minute words with Edith.

"You look lovely, my dear. Do enjoy yourself. Don't worry a mite about me or Danny."

"You're sure you feel up to it?" Susan asked.

"After I put him to bed, I'll do nothing more than sit on this sofa. I'm fine. Still a bit weak, but not so I can't watch this young man."

"I'm gonna be a fine man when I grow up," Danny said. "Like Zack."

"You can't get better than that," Edith said.

Susan silently concurred.

The restaurant Zack took her to was Italian. She savored the aroma of the food when she first stepped in the lobby. "You knew Italian was my favorite, didn't you?" she asked.

"I figured, knowing your mother's Italian. I love Mediterranean cooking. That's one of the things I miss in the Middle East."

They were seated at a small table for two. It was quiet and intimate. The gleaming silverware and crystal sparkled in the subdued lighting. Susan felt like a princess.

The menus were so huge when opened she could not see over hers to Zack. Deciding on the angel hair pasta primavera, she closed it to gaze at Zack. He had already decided on the veal. When their orders had been taken, and wine brought to the table, he proposed a toast.

"To the future, may it give us all we want," he said gravely.

She touched the rim of her glass to his and smiled. "And what is all you want?" she asked after taking a sip.

"A home, a family, a good living and happiness."

"Tall order."

"Do you think so?"

Susan set her glass down carefully and considered her answer. "Maybe not. My parents are still enjoying being married to each other after thirty years. I had a wonderful home life and consider I have a good living now. And Danny makes me so happy." She looked at him.

"As a child, I missed out. No family ties. Not even long-term foster care. I lived in four homes from age four until I turned eighteen. Then I was on my own."

"I thought you said you were still in touch with one family."

"As in we exchange Christmas cards. They've invited me to visit. But I've never gone. They were great, but they aren't blood kin."

"You know what they say—you can choose your friends, but you're stuck with your family. Not being blood kin isn't so bad. There are lots of families and extended families where people aren't related who share their lives. Look at Edith. She's like a devoted aunt to me and Danny. And my parents have friends whom I still see even though we are a generation apart."

Zack was silent for a moment. Now would be the time for her to mention she had adopted Danny and adored him. When she didn't say anything else, he asked "Do you consider blood ties important?"

"Of course. I'm only saying there are other ways to create a family. Look at all the kids who get adopted. Don't you think they're considered part of that family? Or the adopt-a-grandparent project— older people who don't have family and younger ones who need the influence and love older people can give. Some close friends are like family. My aunt Marge and Uncle George aren't blood relatives, but they are closer to us than my mother's sister who lives in North Carolina."

Zack took another sip of his wine and then looked at her. Should he tell her now—that he knew Danny was adopted. And how he knew? He took a breath, and did not.

"I can see your point. But in my case, I have very limited family. I think it's time to put down roots."

She smiled. "That's probably the goal of almost everyone. People marry, have families and want the best for their children. Not everyone, fortunately, ends up in foster care. Roots anchor us, give us a base to always connect to."

"Which is why I want to be there for my child, or children. Things have changed recently. My carefree, footloose days are over. It's time to settle down." He waited for her to confide in him, but she just smiled.

Their salads arrived and Zack used the interruption to change the subject. It was too soon to push for complete revelation. Yet he was growing closer to Susan each time they were together. Could he do as he said—give up his nomadic ways? He had felt alone all his life. Would that change if he married and had a hand in raising Danny?

"Tell me about growing up in New York. How different is it from Chicago? We had the lake, you have the rivers. We had snow, N.Y. has snow. You have Broadway, but we have the Magnificent Mile."

"I was raised in the Upper East Side. We had a nice flat. A park not too far away and a view of the river. Of course, it was between two tall buildings, so a very limited view, but my folks were proud of our sliver of river view. Lots of kids in the building. My best friend, Mary Jane, grew up in the same building. She's with the Peace Corps now in Nigeria. But we're inseparable when she's home. She's like family." Susan grinned at him. "Tell me about your favorite foster home."

"The one where the husband died too young. The Zumwalts were wonderful. He really liked children and played with us every evening after work—even in winter. He said we need not be afraid of the dark, just adapt to lack of light. So we played games like hide-and-seek after dark."

Susan watched as memories came to his mind. He seemed to enjoy remembering the happy times he had with that family. How tragic to lose his biological family and then be wrenched from the foster care that had proved so loving.

"Danny enjoyed playing ball with you. You've been good for him. He needs to see how men are. Mostly he's in a feminine world with me and Edith and his preschool teachers to interact with," Susan said.

"He needs a father figure," Zack said slowly. "Do you think little boys need a male role model more than little girls?"

"Maybe. Or maybe they both need that. Isn't that why normally families have a father and a mother? Each brings something special to the child and balance to a family."

Susan sat back in her chair, wondering if this talk of family was what Zack wanted. This date was to be for the two of them. To enjoy the evening and being with each other.

She smiled wryly. "Guess I'm passionate about families, huh? Tell me more about your work. However did you get into a field that takes you from home so long?"

Zack began to talk about his interest in building,

how in college he gravitated toward structural engineering and the path that led him to the work he'd spent more than a decade doing. He painted a picture Susan could readily see about living in deserts with substandard housing and infrastructures until his company built roads and bridges to facilitate transportation and the beginnings of towns with community buildings and office buildings.

Susan enjoyed listening to him, hearing about the travels he'd done when he got leave. It was fun to explore London and Copenhagen through his memories. He even talked about some of his friends. He seemed to have only a few, but they were mentioned frequently when he talked.

She wanted to know more about the land mine, but hesitated to bring it up in case it shattered the mood. How frightening to be going about a normal workday and be injured so severely? And to have a co-worker die.

When the meal ended, the conversation continued.

"Will you miss it if you settle in the States?" she asked, sipping on the after dinner coffee.

"I think I've put in enough time. I'm looking forward to a more normal lifestyle now—home every night, weekends free."

"Home-cooked meals," she inserted with a laugh.

"If they are as good as yours. Your mother must have taught you well."

"I'll tell her that."

CHAPTER SEVEN

SUNDAY Susan slept in late, tired from the work at the preschool and the late night. Zack had brought her home around midnight. Edith had been asleep on the sofa and Susan hadn't known whether to waken her or let her sleep. Since she looked comfortable enough, Susan left her.

Danny woke her after nine. She smiled at her son as he bounced on her bed. When she moved to get up, she stifled a groan. Her shoulders ached. Flexing her hands, she realized her right hand did as well. Painting demanded muscles not normally used in her regular day.

"Edith is sleeping," Danny whispered.

"I got home late last night. She's probably tired from watching you," Susan said, tickling her son.

His laugher rang out. "Can I wake her up, too?" he asked.

"Not yet. Get a book from your room and you can read in my bed while I take a quick shower. Then if she's still asleep, you can wake her up."

Twenty minutes later when they entered the living room, the sofa was empty. Coffee brewed in the kitchen but when Susan entered, that room was also empty. Probably Edith was grateful to escape before Danny could have wakened her.

Knowing Edith was still recovering from her illness, Susan wanted to give her as much a break as she could. As soon as breakfast was finished, she took Danny to the park. He ran and played with the other children, scooting down the slide, swooshing high on the swing. Susan watched, glad for the chance to sit in the sun and just relax. Soon enough she'd be at the preschool doing some other task she didn't feel suited for.

Glancing at her watch, she saw it was getting close to twelve-thirty. Zack had told her last night he'd pick her up again to walk to the preschool together. She smiled as she remembered their date. The food had been spectacular. But it was the company she loved the most. They'd talked until the restaurant shut down. Then, instead of taking a cab back home, he'd asked if she'd like to walk. She knew the distance, but it would give them more time together, so she'd said yes.

Ambling along, they looked into shop windows and speculated about inhabitants of the apartment buildings they passed. The streets held little traffic that late and it was nice to feel cocooned from cares as they walked and talked. He'd refused to come in when they reached her apartment, but the kiss they'd shared had unsettled her enough it was hard to fall asleep.

She was falling for Zack. The delight she felt every time she saw him was gradually healing her heart. She enjoyed being with him. She'd never expected to fall in love after her husband's death. But then, she'd never anticipated meeting a man like Zack. A man who seemed to enjoy her company—and that of her son.

Any future she envisioned with a man would have to include Danny. She'd want him to learn to love her son as much as she did. To be willing to be father to the boy throughout his life. To promise never to die before they were old and infirmed.

She knew that last bit was impossible. Tom would never have willingly left them. Would Zack? She couldn't imagine living such a carefree life as he'd known, and then changing so drastically to be part of a typical family, going to work five days a week and doing family tasks on the weekends.

Still, a small part of her began to imagine that Zack did fall in love with her. And she with him. They'd marry and have a wonderful life together. He already liked Danny—maybe more than liked. Why else would he plan activities that included her son? And volunteer his time to help repair the preschool? It was not a come-on to lure the mother. She recognized a growing bond between the two of them.

On the other hand, Zack might be finding this situation novel. He could test drive his commitment to changing after the land mine and see if it were something he'd like. There was nothing stopping him from taking off tomorrow and returning to the Middle East and projects that demanded all his skill and knowledge.

His leaving would break her heart. She swallowed, tears filling her eyes. She was falling for Zack Morgan. And didn't have a clue what to do about it. How could she guard herself and her son from hurt if Zack suddenly decided to leave?

She couldn't. It was already too late. She could only go forward and hope she wasn't making a mistake that would make both her and Danny miserable for years to come.

Zack found his pace quickening as he turned onto Susan's block. Up ahead he could see her and Danny about to enter the apartment building. She must have taken him to the park. At least Danny would sleep part of the afternoon, making it easier on Edith. Zack knew from the days he'd watched his son that the boy seemed to possess the energy of a battalion of men.

And he wouldn't change a single thing about him.

As if attuned to his presence, Susan turned around and looked. Her smile when she saw him could light up the street, Zack thought as he locked his gaze with hers and walked even faster.

"Zack!" Danny ran down the three steps and raced down the sidewalk toward him, his face beaming in happiness.

Zack picked him up when Danny reached him and swung him high in the air. The little boy laughed aloud. Zack heard Susan's laughter at the same time. For a moment he could scarcely move. He felt truly and completely happy for the first time in years. This felt right.

"Hi," Susan called, coming a few feet down the sidewalk to meet him.

"Hi yourself," he said. Holding Danny with one arm, he drew her closer with the other and kissed her. Not as long as he wanted, but they were on a public street and Danny was only about six inches away.

"Kiss me, too," Danny said, putting his hands on Zack's cheeks and turning his head to face him.

Zack smiled and kissed his plump cheek.

"I'm happy to see you both," he said, his gaze going back to Susan's.

Did he imagine it, or was the sadness so often evident in her eyes gone?

"Ready to work again?"

"I'm so stiff from yesterday. But I'm game," she said as they walked toward the apartment.

"I feel the same way, but it's a good feeling. I'm

back in my stride now and want to see if I can get off medical leave sooner than I thought. I'm calling the company's medical doctor on Monday to see when he can see me."

Susan tried to smile, but the anxiety that clutched at her was too strong. If Zack was pronounced ready to return to work, he'd have no reason to remain in New York. Granted, he'd talked about setting down roots. But with the next breath, he'd talked about his foreign assignments and she could hear how much he liked his work.

Where did that leave her?

What did she want? In one thought, she believed shc'd never love another like Tom. In another, the idea of Zack leaving, maybe never to be seen again, filled her with anguish. She had come to care for him much more than she realized. The thought of his leaving filled her with panic.

She needed some time to consider all the ramifications. Now it didn't look as if she was going to get what she wanted.

They dropped Danny off with Edith and headed for the school.

"You're really quiet today," Zack said as they walked side by side.

"Sorry. It's really wonderful you feel fully recovered and can return to work."

"But?"

She looked at him. "But what?"

"I don't know, it just sounded like a but should be in there somewhere."

"But I'll miss you," she blurted out.

He slung his arm across her shoulder and drew her closer. "Hey, getting a release just means I'm in working shape again. I told you I'm thinking of looking for something here in the States."

"America is awfully big," she said. "In the States could mean Alaska, which is just about as far from here as the Middle East."

"Don't want me so far away, huh?"

She shook her head, facing forward. The school was in sight. One of the other parents waved and Susan tried to smile as she waved back. She wanted to cry instead.

Zack wasn't sure what to make of Susan's statement. He admitted to himself he wanted her to give him some indication of her feelings for him. Should he suggest staying? Or wait for her to suggest that?

What if she didn't?

He nodded at the other parents as they filed into the old building. The men he'd worked with yesterday greeted him. It felt good to be part of a community effort. He had friends at the work sites, but no one with a normal home life. These men had routine jobs, went home to their families each evening and were working to better circumstances for their children.

"We were thinking of getting together after

today's work to celebrate one weekend down," Brad Singleton said as he and Zack started on replacing the last of the drywall in one classroom. "Join us?"

"Sounds like fun. I'll have to check with Susan."

"Yeah, baby-sitters can be a pain. If yours can't stay, bring the kid."

"You bringing yours?"

"We have Betsy's niece staying with us this weekend to watch the rugrats. We'll take her to school in the morning and she'll go home from there, so no worries on our end."

"Lucky." Zack reached for his hammer and began to pound nails. How normal and ordinary the conversation was. Yet for him—extraordinary. If he stayed, if he could build a life with Susan, he would have many encounters like this. Be part of a community that pulled together when things needed doing.

He and Brad talked as they worked and before four, they had finished the second classroom's walls.

"Time for mud and then next week these walls can be painted," he said.

"Jason is the expert on that," Brad said.

"Good, because I'm not," Zack replied.

"But you seem expert in every other aspect."

He grinned. "Well I worked construction through college, and have been on job sites ever since."

"Building a bridge isn't exactly the same thing as repairing a preschool," Brad said.

"We sometimes have to build our own homes while we are on a job site, so I can handle a smattering of plumbing, wiring and drywall."

"Man, you've really lived an exciting life."

Zack shrugged. "It was what I wanted. Now things have changed."

"Susan?" Brad asked as they walked over to Mrs. Hampton's office for the next assignment.

Zack hesitated a minute, glancing at Brad. The question caused him to clarify his feelings. The entire reason he was thinking of changing his lifestyle was because of Susan. The thought kicked him in the gut. He'd been stunned when he received the letter about his son, but had convinced himself once he knew the boy was well cared for, he'd move on and let him have the love and security of his adoptive parents.

Meeting Susan had changed all that. For the first time since he was a kid he began to think about family ties, facing the world united as a couple, leaving his nomadic ways and becoming a man who put down roots and made a difference in a community.

If Susan was there. She made a man long to have her smile at him when he came home at night. Share life's ups and downs. And make a warm and loving home where they could shut away the world and be in a world of their own. Their last kiss flashed into his mind. He couldn't imagine not kissing her. Not having the right to kiss her if she turned to someone else.

"Yeah, I guess because of Susan," he admitted aloud.

"That's cool, man. My sister has three kids and her dead-beat husband left several years ago. She can hardly get a date because of those children. Most men don't want to get involved," Brad said.

"I don't have a lot of experience with kids. Or women, for that matter. Don't you think it would be a privilege to be part of a child's life?" Zack asked.

"Well, of course I do. I have two children myself and can't imagine life without them. Not all men think like that, however."

Zack knew that. Before he'd met Susan, and Danny, he'd been one of them. The thought filled him with panic. He'd been alone most of his life. Now he craved a woman who was still grieving her lost husband.

Mrs. Harper had a large sheet spread out over a table beside her desk. She was leaning over it checking on tasks yet to be done when the two men entered her office.

"Room two complete," Brad said. "What next?"

She looked up and smiled. "This is going so much faster than I anticipated. At this rate, we may finish in only a couple of weekends. The painting is complete in Mrs. Savalack's room. Mrs. Rosa's room and Mrs. Thompkin's rooms now are ready for the next stage. We have the ceilings to repair in two rooms, but there are parents already there. Are you two up for the playground equipment?"

"What's needed?" Zack asked.

"Some of the older equipment is made of wood. It's splintered and deteriorating. It needs to be replaced, bolted in place and then finished so it's safe for the children. And we had two new plastic climbing jungle gyms donated that have to be assembled."

"Zack will be perfect for that—he's used to building bridges. How hard can some playground equipment be?" Brad said.

Mrs. Harper studied him for a moment, smiling in gratitude. "We are fortunate, indeed, to have you helping, Mr. Morgan."

"Zack, please. I'll look at what you have. We already picked up the lumber, right?"

"Yes, it was in the original order you were so helpful in acquiring for us."

As the men headed out to the playground area, Brad asked about the order. Zack explained about the company's policy of helping in local communities.

"That's why those other two guys were here yesterday?" Brad asked.

"Right. They'll be back next Saturday, too."

The entire property in front of the old building was enclosed by a wrought-iron fence. There was a separate area for the playground from the front walkway, and the playground was cross fenced. The double walkway that led from the sidewalk to the front door also had a gate, but it was rusted open.

"If it had been closed that day," Zack said, going

to examine it more closely, "Danny would never have been able to run off like he did."

"What's happened?" Brad had not heard the story. When Zack finished, he looked at Zack. "If he hadn't run off, you would never have met Susan and end up here helping out. Sounds like fate to me."

Zack nodded as he assessed what was needed to get the gates in working order again. He had initially planned only to walk down the street, check out the preschool and see if his son was in the playground. He had not planned to stop or introduce himself. He'd never expected to have Susan ask for his help. Maybe it was fate. Did that auger for a positive spin on his idea of family?

"This has rusted pretty good. But I think if we can get it off the hinges and use a solvent to get to bare metal, we can paint and lubricate so it'll work for years." He glanced at Brad.

"Hey, man, I'm up for anything to keep the kids safer. This is a dangerous world and this isn't the best neighborhood. Just the best we can afford," Brad said.

Zack knew that was true for Susan as well. If they married, he could easily afford to establish them in a better neighborhood in New York City, or even move out to Long Island where they could have a house with a big yard. He paused a moment to try to imagine himself a home owner. It was not something he'd thought about since he'd been a child and had planned to buy the biggest house he could and never leave it.

Obviously the dream had changed as he grew up, but now he wondered if it had just lurked in the back of his mind all these years. He could picture the exact kind of house he wanted.

"Need help?" Brad asked.

Zack looked at the gate he was holding. He struggled a bit to lift it from the hinges and Brad stepped in to help. Together they wrested it from the supports and laid the gate on the walkway. In only moments, with the help of some well placed blows from a hammer, they had the second gate off as well.

"Not in our job descriptions, but something that needs doing," Zack said, studying the rusted hinges. Years of experience paid off; he knew metals and how to care for them. In only a half hour, he and Brad had stripped the rust from each hinge and lightly brushed the gates with a wire brush in preparation for the first coat of paint.

"This will have to do until next workday—we didn't buy wrought-iron paint," Zack said. Maybe he could get some tomorrow and come back during the week. He had nothing else to do until his medical leave ended.

"It's almost five. We'll be winding up soon," Brad said.

"Let's put these back up. I can get them down to paint later," Zack said.

When the gates were back in place, they opened and closed with no effort. When closed, the center latch kept them in place.

Cleaning up the area, Zack returned the tools to the staging area and went to hunt for Susan. He found her with several other mothers, cleaning paintbrushes in one of the bathrooms, the door propped open for ventilation.

He waited opposite the door, listening to the female chatter. The topic was children. He figured he could never learn too much about that so listened as they discussed eating patterns and how to get them to eat enough vegetables. He felt a spurt of pride in Danny. The child never argued with Susan about what to eat. Her nutritious meals were delicious as well as healthful.

She glanced up at one point and looked directly at him. The smile that lit her face reminded him of why he was here. She was not good at hiding her emotions. He nodded, but said nothing.

She murmured something to the woman next to her, who then looked over at him.

"We've been asked to join the others for dinner, can you make it?" she called.

He nodded once, glad the day wasn't going to end soon. He enjoyed being with Susan and the other parents. Samuel at the job site would split a gut laughing if he could see him now. Zack didn't care. This was uncharted territory for him, and he was interested in exploring every facet.

"We're going as is—no one wants to go home first and change," she said, rinsing her hands and then drying them with a paper towel. One of the other mothers gathered all the brushes and shook them in the deep sink, then wrapped them in plastic bags.

Susan came out to the hall, rotating her shoulders a bit. "I won't be able to move tomorrow," she said.

"Turn around," Zack said, and when she complied, he gently massaged her shoulders and neck.

"Ohhh, that feels heavenly," she said, letting her head fall forward.

"Lucky you. Wish Jim would think of something like that for me," the red-haired mother said in passing. "Or I could stand in line and get a turn?" she teased.

Zack grinned at her. "You'd have to ask Susan."

"Hmmm," she said, not offering to share.

The redhead laughed and continued down the hall. Soon Zack and Susan were alone.

"Do we go?" he said, enjoying the feel of her slight frame in his hands. Her muscles were tense, but he gently worked on them to loosen them up. He knew she wasn't used to this kind of work.

"We go," she said with a sigh. Stepping away, she turned. "Thank you, that feels wonderful."

He leaned over and kissed her.

"That feels wonderful," he said.

In only moments they were out front with the others. Mrs. Harper was opening and closing the gate in delight.

"This is wonderful. We can keep the children in no matter what, and keep out those we don't want wandering in."

Susan looked at Zack. "Did you fix that?"

"I remember Danny running away. What if another child did—without the quick find. It wasn't hard to do."

"But not even on the list of things to repair. As a grateful mother, thank you."

"Brad pointed out that if it had been fixed before, I wouldn't have met you," Zack said.

Her eyes widened at that.

"I can't imagine not knowing you," she said involuntarily

"Hold that thought for later," he said.

The group who went to dinner together chose to walk to the same pizza place Zack had taken Susan and Danny.

They crowded around two tables pushed together. The conversation was lively and full of laughter. Parents told stories about their children. They all lauded the work of the preschool. And twice Zack was asked about his own work and how he'd come to volunteer with their group. He found the evening entertaining. He laughed with the others, and kept glancing at Susan. She seemed to be enjoying herself as well.

When they walked home, it was by themselves. He reached out to take her hand, linking their fingers.

"Tired?" he asked.

"Yes. I sure wish I didn't have to go to work tomorrow. I'd love to take a hot bath before bed and then sleep in until noon."

"Take a day off," he suggested.

"No, I have to save my time in case Danny gets sick or something."

"You wouldn't have to do that if you stayed home with him, would you?" Zack said slowly.

"No, but that's not possible."

"It would be if you had a husband to take care of earning the income while you took care of Danny. And the husband, of course," he said, testing the waters. His gaze was fixed on her as they walked. She stared straight ahead.

"But I don't have a husband."

"You would if you marry me."

At Susan's stunned look, Zack began to backpedal.

"Just think about it. No need to answer now." God, how could he have made such a blunder. He hadn't even told her of his relationship to her son. She hadn't confided in him about Danny. They really hardly knew each other.

But he knew down in his gut that marrying Susan would give him all he wanted in life. Had his impetuous proposal ruined everything?

CHAPTER EIGHT

Susan stumbled, grabbed hold of Zack and stared at him in astonishment.

"What did you say?"

"I was going to wait. I should take you out to dinner and maybe a carriage ride around Central Park after dark. That would be more romantic. But it just came out. I know you never thought about it. But think about it now, okay? Just think about it. Don't say no right away."

She listened to him, amazed she could concentrate when her heart raced so. Zack had just asked her to marry him! She didn't know what to say. She kept quiet as he kept explaining away the casual comment as they walked alone. He'd planned to ask her. He'd actually thought about what would be romantic and had planned it. This wasn't some knee-jerk reaction to the thought of her having to work.

At first she couldn't speak. No, was her initial response. Automatic. I love Tom!

But as she watched Zack grow more and more flustered as he tried to explain, her heart blossomed. She had worried about his leaving. Now he was asking her to marry him, to make a home with him.

Suddenly she realized he had stopped talking and was watching her closely.

"Are you all right?" he asked.

"Surprised," she said. Slowly she released the grip on his arm, smoothed the wrinkled shirt watching as she did so, trying to get her reeling senses under control and find an answer. Yes or no? Keep him forever in her life or refuse to share hers with him?

"We haven't known each other long," she began. Don't let me make a mistake here, she prayed.

"You're right. Forget it. It was too soon." He turned and took a step.

Susan remained where she was.

"Forget it? Did you or did you not ask me to marry you?"

He turned, tilting his head slightly as he studied her. "I did. Badly, but I did."

"I never expected to get married again."

"Why not? You're young and pretty and fun to be with. And you have an adorable child who needs a father."

She nodded. "A lot of men don't want to raise someone else's child."

"I'm not a lot of men." He looked back toward the preschool. "I enjoyed working at Danny's school, using talents I have for something besides earning a living. That's a good group of people, working to make life better for their children." *Tell her,* something inside urged. *She needs to know.*

"That's certain." She glanced at him, glanced away. "I'm not sure I can give you an answer right now."

"Let's keep on as we've been and see what develops," he suggested. *Tell her, tell her.*

She met his gaze. "I won't ever forget. You caught me by surprise, that's all."

He nodded. Taking a deep breath, he turned. Soon they were both walking back to the apartment. Susan knew she'd disappointed him. He'd obviously been thinking about this for a while and had obviously hoped she'd immediately accept.

Why hadn't she? The last weeks had been special. Zack was special. Why was she hesitating? He'd had more excitement in his life than she'd ever see, yet was willing to settle down with her and make a family. At least, that's what she thought.

"Do you plan to quit working abroad?" she asked.

"Yes. I wouldn't marry and leave you," he said.

"Settle here or back in Chicago?" she asked.

"Here. Or in the vicinity at least. I was thinking maybe something in Long Island. I'd like to be near the water after all the desert living I've done. But I'm flexible."

Susan looked ahead, seeing her apartment building in the distance. If she married Zack, it would mean drastic changes. Moving from this neighborhood would not be a problem. It worried her that Danny would have to grow up here. But to marry Zack, make a home with him? It would be different from anything she'd expected.

The question remained: Would she be happy with Zack?

Yes!

So what was the problem? Danny? Zack seemed to enjoy being with him as much as with her. And Danny clearly adored Zack. Would they be a perfect match?

She cleared her throat. "Actually you haven't seen Danny when he throws a temper tantrum. He can be less than endearing sometimes."

Zack looked at her. The words ready to be spoken. Would it make a difference? Instead he said, "All kids throw temper tantrums. That doesn't change how we feel about them. Are you worried I won't love him?" *He's my son, I'll always love him.*

"No. I…you caught me by surprise, that's all. Give me a couple of days, please? I don't want to make a spur-of-the-moment decision."

They reached the apartment building.

"I won't come in," Zack said, looking down the street. "I need to get back to the hotel.

"Come tomorrow for dinner?" she asked.

He looked down at her. "How about I treat you to that dinner and carriage ride?"

She smiled. "I'd like that." Reaching up, she brushed her lips against his. "I may even have an answer for you by then." Turning, Susan ran up the three stairs to the lobby and into the apartment building. She hugged Danny when she entered. Looking at Edith, she longed to share the situation, but kept silent. This was one decision she had to make on her own.

Later Susan took a long hot bath to ease tense muscles. She closed her eyes, remembering Zack massaging her shoulders. She wished he were here now. She could use an all-over body massage.

Which she could get if they married.

She sat up, feeling breathless. He'd really asked her to marry him. What was there to debate? She loved him. She longed to be with him, to hear him speak, watch his eyes when they lighted in amusement, or turned soft when kissing her.

He was a good man. Steady and reliable.

He was a stranger. Someone she'd bumped into the day Danny had run away from preschool.

His actions were sound. He could have said no he hadn't seen the child and moved on. Instead everything he'd done had been helpful.

And his kisses were wonderful. She smiled in remembrance. She wouldn't mind a few more of those right now.

How would Danny react to having Zack become part of their family?

How would her parents? Ohmygosh, she'd have to call them in the morning and clue them in that she was considering—marrying Zack Morgan. A man they had never met.

She was truly considering marrying Zack. It took a moment for the truth to sink in. She should have said yes on the sidewalk. If he changed his mind, she'd die.

She loved him. Once she went beyond thinking there would only be one man in her life, she knew Zack was the man for her now.

They would have a short engagement, she hoped. She couldn't wait to start their family life together. Laughing in glee, she sank to her chin, smiling in delight. She was going to marry Zack Morgan.

First thing the next morning Susan called her parents.

"Is everything okay, dear," her mother asked. "It's early for a call. We missed Saturday's chat. How did the work at the preschool go?"

"Everything's fine, Mom. We accomplished more than the headmistress thought we would. And I received a proposal of marriage."

"That's nice, I'm glad—wait! Did you say you got a proposal? For marriage?"

Susan heard her father's exclamation in the background.

"From Zack Morgan. I think I mentioned him before."

"Mentioned is all. I had no idea you were so involved. Isn't this sudden?"

"A bit. But I'm sure. He's sure. You'll like him, Mom. He's steady and thoughtful." And sexy, but she wasn't sure that was something her mother would want to hear. "And he's very good with Danny."

"You aren't marrying him because he likes Danny, are you?" her mother asked sharply.

"No, Mom. I'm marrying Zack because I love him. Very much. And I hope you and Dad will as well. But it won't matter in the end. It matters only that I love him."

"Your father and I will be up next weekend to meet this young man. We can discuss wedding preparations then."

"I hadn't thought about a wedding. I had such a fairy-tale one with Tom. I don't need another. We can get married at a judge's chambers."

"Is this Zack's first marriage?"

"Yes."

"Then maybe he needs one," her mother suggested gently.

"Oh. You're right. Though, he may not want one. He has no family. He was raised in foster homes."

"But he has a good job?"

"He's a structural engineer and for the last decade has worked major projects in the Middle East. Now he's going to settle down here and find something that will allow him to come home every night. He wants to buy a home in Long Island."

"This seems so sudden."

"I know, he caught me by surprise, too. Tonight he's taking me to dinner and a carriage ride in the park. We'll have lots to discuss." She counted the minutes until she'd see him again.

"Keep me posted. We'll take the ten o'clock flight from Orlando and get there in the early afternoon Saturday."

"We're still scheduled for preschool work. Edith will be here with Danny."

"So your Zack is helping at the preschool renovations."

"He's been a major help. He got all the materials donated by his company, brought a couple of other engineers to help the first day and works harder and faster than any of the parents who've shown up."

"I like the way you stand up for him. Shows you care."

"Of course I do. I love Zack." The more she said it, the more Susan wondered why she had doubts. She loved him and could envision a long, happy life together.

Susan was scarcely able to concentrate at work. She kept watching the time. Did the clock hands always move so slowly? She wanted to see Zack. Tell him her answer. Discuss their future and kiss him silly.

Finally. She had dashed home, changed into another dress and freshened her makeup. Brushing her hair, she let it fall down her back in waves. A touch of perfume and she was ready.

Edith had agreed to watch Danny. Susan didn't know what she'd do without Edith. Which brought up the question of what would Edith do when they moved?

Some of her happiness dimmed. For two years Edith had stepped in as a surrogate grandmother, watching Danny, helping Susan. She'll be lost, Susan thought.

She went into the living room to visit with Edith until Zack arrived. When he knocked on the door, Danny ran for it, stopping and yelling, "Who is it?" He put his ear against the door. Satisfied with the answer, he opened it.

"I waited until you said Zack," he told the man proudly.

"Good job." Zack smiled at him, his gaze immediately searching for Susan. She rose and came to greet him.

"You look beautiful," he said, taking in her dress and shoes.

"You look wonderful," she murmured, suddenly feeling shy. How did a newly-almost-engaged woman greet her soon to be fiancé?

"You two have a good dinner," Edith said, waving at Zack from the sofa.

"Can I go?" Danny said, clinging to Zack's leg.

"Not this time. You would be bored at the restaurant I've chosen. I hope your mom will like it, though," Zack said.

Susan did. It was the Tavern on the Green. A delightful restaurant in the heart of Central Park. With dining inside and out, it was lit with thousands of tiny lights. It looked like a fairyland.

They were shown a table near the windows, inside where it was warm, but with an unobstructive view of the outside.

Zack ordered champagne and when it had been delivered offered a toast. "To us."

"To us," Susan repeated, the rim of her flute touching his.

Zack said nothing more about his proposal, but proceeded to tell her about calling for a medical release and getting an appointment two weeks from now. "I wanted to be released immediately. I guess to the company, two weeks is immediately."

"So you'll be here for another two weeks, at least."

"Plenty of time to finish the preschool renovations. I talked with Mrs. Harper and I can go over some afternoons when they'll combine classes to give me room to work."

"That's great. But shouldn't you take advantage of the two weeks left to rest up?"

"I'll only be working four hours a day. Hardly enough to give me a problem." His dark eyes gazed into hers. "Tell me about your day."

"I called my parents. They are flying up this weekend to meet you."

"I thought we were working at the preschool."

"I told my mom that. They'll go right to the apartment and visit with Danny until we get there."

"Maybe I'll bring a change of clothes to the school," Zack said.

She laughed. "I think they'll excuse messy clothes knowing you've been helping at their grandson's school. In fact, they'll love you to death for being so nice to me and Danny."

"And you?"

"I'll love you to death, too," she said seriously.

He raised his glass to hers and they both drank a sip.

As soon as dinner was finished, Zack steered them to the carriage ride concession. They climbed aboard and were tucked in with a lap robe. It was cool in the evenings. As the horse started its rounds, Zack pulled Susan closer and kissed her.

"Susan, will you marry me?" he asked seriously when he ended the kiss.

"Yes, I will be very happy to marry you," she replied, reaching up to kiss him again.

She felt giddy and excited and a bit scared. Not about her relationship with Zack, but the fact life came with no guarantees. She hoped they'd have fifty or sixty years together—even more. But she'd take whatever time they did have together and relish every moment. She refused to take anything for granted again.

Zack couldn't believe she'd said yes. After her reaction yesterday, he was sure he'd blown it. He wanted to tell the world. Which, of course, they would do when they got the marriage license and could get married.

"How soon?" he asked.

She laughed. "Soon. I can't wait to be your wife. And have you all to myself every night."

"Not as much as I want you for my wife. I will have to fly back to the Middle East to wind things up. Shouldn't take more than a few days. I've told the company I'm not returning even when I get the medical release. They're searching for a replacement for me."

"You're giving up a lot," she said.

"No, nothing worth keeping. Not compared to what I'm getting."

"Danny's going to be thrilled," she said. "I didn't tell him. I thought we should be together to do that."

"It's too late tonight," Zack said. It was already past nine and Danny went to bed at eight. "Tomorrow? I can come over after you finish work."

"Perfect."

"Once we're finished with the preschool projects, I'd like to start looking for a place for us. Any preferences?"

"Just close to transit. I do not want to have to drive into the city every day."

"I thought you might like to stay home with Danny. Maybe even consider having more children."

She tried to see him in the dark. His eyes were focused on her.

"It was what I wanted before. I stayed home until I had to go to work when—" She stopped so suddenly Zack knew she'd been about to mention Tom.

"It's okay to talk about him. He was your husband for several years, an important part of your life. Before now." He refused to be jealous of a man dead two years. But he wished he could have been first in Susan's life. He had to settle for being last.

"Now, you are the important part of my life," she said. "I would love to stay home with Danny, at least until he's in school. And if we have other children, I'd want to be home with them when they're young. Then I can decide what to do. I could teach German, you know. If I got a teacher's job, I'd be home when Danny had school breaks."

"You decide. I have enough money that whatever you want is fine."

"I'm worried about Edith," she said slowly.

"Why?"

"She's been such a help to me these last two

years, but I've also helped her with the baby-sitting money. She has a very small pension and with prices rising, it's tough."

"Maybe another family will move into your apartment and need her services."

"Maybe. If I keep working, maybe she could get an apartment near us and continue to watch Danny."

"You'd go back to work just to keep her employed?" he asked.

"I like my job, actually. And he'll be in school before long. It's hard to leave her—she's part of the family."

Zack thought about it for a moment. Edith was part of Susan's extended family. She cared more for the woman than as a mere baby-sitter. "Maybe we can find a home with one of those in-law units. Edith could move with us. And be available when you and I want to get away."

Susan beamed at him. "That's a brilliant solution. So you're thinking you and I might want to get away?"

"For dinner some nights. Maybe a few weekends in the city to see a play or something. But I don't plan to be gone from home and family for more than a few days at a time. I'm going to want you all to myself," Zack said, and pulled her closer for another kiss.

The carriage ride was a dream. Zack couldn't believe she'd said yes. The only doubt was telling her about his relationship to Danny. Should he do it now? Or wait until she confessed he was adopted?

She had to know. He had to tell her. But the ride was as romantic as he could get. He didn't want to shatter the moment.

He had the hurdle of meeting her parents and passing their inquisition. But even if they didn't approve, he would push to get his way. He wanted Susan more than he ever expected. The future would be bleak indeed if he lost her and Danny.

Susan was almost floating as they returned to her apartment. They had discussed getting married in June, less than six weeks away. Zack hadn't been that sold on a formal wedding, but remembering what her mother had said, Susan suggested a small wedding in a chapel. She would splurge for a new dress and maybe a picture-book hat with a small veil. She wanted to always remember this wedding as special—as special as the man she was marrying.

"I can't wait until we tell Danny," she said as they rode up the elevator. "He's going to be thrilled, I know it.

Edith greeted them and then looked at them both closely. "Something's up," she commented.

"We're getting married," Susan said with a rush, then went to hug her friend. "Be happy for us."

"I'm delighted," Edith said, returning her hug. Then she looked at Zack. "Take good care of this woman…she's very special."

"I will. With your help. We'd like you to consider

moving when we do. We're going to look for a house with an in-law unit."

"Oh, my." Edith looked as flustered as Susan had felt when Zack first proposed. "It's so unexpected. Are you sure?"

"His proposal was unexpected, and we're both sure—about getting married and having you move with us. Danny and I will still need you."

"Oh my." The older woman gave a tremulous smile. "I'd be delighted."

She extended her good wishes to them both and left.

Zack glanced at his watch. "It's after eleven," he said, pulling her into his arms again. "I don't want to go, but you have to get up for work tomorrow."

She snuggled closer, savoring his strong arms around her, the beat of his heart against hers. She felt cherished. It had been a long time on her own. She loved this man, loved being half of a couple. She hated to say good-night.

"So before long, you and I won't have to say good-night and part," he said, practically reading her mind. Or was it he felt the same?

"I can hardly wait," she said, tipping her face up for another kiss.

The next evening, Susan came home to find Zack had arrived a few minutes ahead of her. He was talking with Edith while Danny played with some toys on the floor of the living room.

"Hi," she said, tossing her purse on the small table and shedding her coat.

Zack smiled that sexy smile of his and rose to cross over to kiss her.

Danny ran to greet her, too. After Zack's kiss, Susan picked Danny up and kissed him on the cheek. "Hello to you, my man. How was your day?" She shifted her gaze to Zack.

"Me and Edith went to the park. I went way high on the swing."

"Good for you."

"I'll be running along. Zack and I had a nice chat. I had best get started weeding through things I don't want to move and getting ready," Edith said.

Once she was gone, Susan carried Danny into the living room and sat down, holding him on her lap.

"Zack and I have something to tell you," she said, smiling at Zack.

"What?" Danny asked.

"We are going to get married. Zack will live with us after that and we'll be a family."

Danny swiveled around and looked at Zack. "Are you my new daddy?"

Zack glanced at Susan, then nodded. "I'll be your new daddy," he said.

Danny looked at his mother. "He doesn't look like Daddy. I have a picture. Zack's not my daddy."

"No, he's not Tom. But when we get married,

he'll be your new daddy," Susan explained. "Your first daddy went to heaven, remember? Now you'll have a second daddy."

"I'll always love you, Danny. You'll see how good I can take care of you and your mommy," Zack said, reaching to ruffle his hair.

"'Kay," Danny said. He struggled to get down and went to play with his toys.

Susan laughed nervously. "I guess it hasn't sunk in yet. Once we're living together, I think he'll understand better."

As Susan prepared the meal that evening she thought about the changes coming. She had never liked the poky little apartment, but it was the best she could afford. Now Zack was talking about moving to Long Island and buying a house with a yard—and in-law unit for Edith. She wouldn't have to work if she didn't want to.

The idea of spending the day with Danny was extremely appealing. She felt she missed so much while away at work. Little children grew at an amazing rate, learning new things every day exploring their world.

One change would be in preschools. For a moment she felt a wave of sadness. The teachers at his preschool had been wonderful. Working on the renovations made her feel a real connection to the goals of the establishment. They would be leaving that behind when moving.

On the other hand, the neighborhood they'd find would be so much safer for children. She'd make sure they looked for a good school district.

Zack helped with putting Danny to bed that evening by reading him his story. When Danny was asleep, Zack returned to the kitchen where Susan was just finishing the dishes.

"He's out like a light," he said, leaning against the doorjamb, watching her. She was graceful in all she did, including dishes. He felt a contentment at the sight. Being with Susan made him happy. They didn't have to go to fancy nightclubs, constantly seek outside entertainment. Just being with her was enough. He liked to watch her, hear her laughter. He hoped he could make her happy. As happy as she was making him.

He wasn't sure he had it in him to be a good father. But he'd watched George Zumwalt. He knew how a good husband cherished his wife. As he cherished Susan.

He'd risk everything for the chance at making a life with Susan.

Susan turned and gave him a mock frown. "You could come help," she said.

He smiled and let his gaze roam over her. "You're handling that like a pro," he teased.

She folded the dish towel and hung it over the rod nearby. "I want a dishwasher in my new house," she said.

"Done."

"His name could be Zack," she said slyly, turning to grin at him.

He laughed. He hadn't been teased in a long time. It felt good.

"Or its name could be Whirlpool or KitchenAid. Especially if you want all your dishes in one piece by the end of the week."

She sashayed across the room, her gaze never leaving his. He could feel his heart rate increase as she drew near. When her toes almost touched his, she put her hands on her hips and tilted back her head. "I think you are better with your hands than that," she said.

He uncrossed his arms and slowly drew her against him. "I would love to prove the point."

He lowered his mouth to hers, giving her a deep kiss that rocked her back on her heels. Her arms encircled his neck and she pressed even closer, relishing every inch of him that touched. She couldn't wait until they were married.

Saturday Zack arrived in time for breakfast and brought croissants and coffee from the coffeehouse near his hotel. Susan had prepared pancakes for Danny and he was licking the syrup from his fork when Zack walked into the kitchen.

"I have pancakes," Danny said.

"So I see. I brought your mommy something

else." He set his bag and tray of coffee on the table. "Ready to paint again?" he asked, kissing her.

"As I'll ever be," Susan said a minute later. "I checked the flights and my parents are still due to arrive midafternoon. I told Mrs. Harper we'd try to cut out early."

When they found a place to live, he hoped the neighbors would be as friendly and accepting as the parents at Danny's preschool. In fact he hoped all the neighbors would become family friends. Susan would blossom in such a setting. He'd need her help to become comfortable, but was making inroads with Brad and the other fathers working on the pre-school projects.

Brad and Betsy Singleton were already at the school when Zack and Susan arrived. Splitting up to go to their separate tasks, Zack watched her walk away. He wished they were working together.

"She's a looker," Brad commented as he watched Zack watching Susan.

"She's agreed to marry me," Zack said quietly. The wonder was still there.

"Hey, man, that's great!" Brad socked him on the arm. "We'll have to celebrate."

In no time everyone helping knew of the new engagement. There were many congratulations, men and women even coming outside to speak with Zack while he and Brad worked on the play-ground equipment. From the comments flying,

Zack knew they were happy for Susan. He was pretty happy himself.

It was after three when he and Susan broke away from the work and headed back to her apartment. He had washed up in the hallway bathroom of the preschool, doing the best he could with limited resources. He wanted to make a good impression on Susan's parents. For a moment he stared at himself in the mirror, remembering back to changing foster houses. He'd always wanted to make a good impression in hopes the people would keep him. It felt almost the same. If her parents didn't approve, would Susan still marry him?

CHAPTER NINE

Susan's parents were at her apartment when Susan and Zack arrived. Edith was talking with them, while Danny sat in his grandma's lap. He struggled off when he spotted his mother.

"Grandma and Poppa are here. They came to visit," he said, jumping up and down. Susan picked him up and gave him a hug. "I see they are. Are you being a good host?"

"What's a host?"

"Someone who has company over. Hi, Mom, Dad."

They had both risen and crossed to greet their daughter and the man who would soon become part of the family.

"This is Zack Morgan. Zack, my parents, Amelia and Tony Molina."

Tony shook Zack's hand. Her mother surprised her by hugging Zack.

"Welcome to our family," she said. "I hope you will always keep my daughter happy."

"I'll do my best," Zack said.

Edith stayed only a little while before leaving. Danny loved being the center of attention and acted up a little until Susan warned him a time-out would be forthcoming if he didn't settle down a little. He looked at Zack.

"Your grandparents are going to be here for a while. There'll be time to spend with just them," he said. Danny nodded and went back to sit in Amelia's lap. Soon he was dozing.

"Edith said he didn't have a nap," Tony said, watching the little boy. "We got here shortly after two—good connections from the airport."

"I'll put him in his bed," Zack said.

Once he'd left the room, Susan looked at her parents. "Well, what do you think?"

"Honey, we just met him. He seems nice, but it'll take a few days to get to know him better," her mother said.

"The question is, what do you think?" her father asked.

"I think he's wonderful. He's patient and kind and is really good with Danny."

"You are not marrying him just to get a father for Danny, are you?"

She shook her head. "No. I'm marrying him for me. It's just a bonus that he wants to be a father to Danny."

When Zack returned, he sat on the sofa beside Susan and looked at her parents.

"Questions, I'm sure."

"How did you two meet?" her mother asked.

For the next hour or so, Zack easily answered all the questions the Molinas asked.

Even when her father asked about his monetary situation and Susan protested.

"I've been working abroad for the last dozen years. The company pays well for hardship locales and provides housing. I've saved quite a bit, and invested it. Susan won't have to worry about money."

"That'll be a switch," Amelia said, glancing around the small room.

"Mom!"

"Will you have to work, or can you stay home with Danny?" her mother asked.

Zack replied, "That's up to Susan. She likes her job, so if she wants to continue, that's fine with me. But I'd be as happy to have her stay home with Danny."

"And any other kids we may have," she said.

They talked about their plans for finding a house. For a small wedding.

"Honeymoon?" her mother asked.

Susan looked at Zack. "We never talked about that."

"We can later," he said. He was getting a bit impatient with all the conversation. What was the verdict? Did the Molinas think he was suitable for their daughter?

Finally her father looked at his watch. "I think

we better head for the hotel and check in, Amelia," he said. "We'll meet for dinner at seven?"

"That'll be fine, Dad," Susan said, rising when he did.

"You're not staying here?" Zack asked, also rising.

"Not enough room. And only one bathroom," Amelia said, standing. "If you buy a house on the Island, do get one with more than one bathroom."

When they'd gone, Zack looked at Susan. "What did they say, anything?"

She went to him, oddly touched at his vulnerability. She always thought of him as invincible. "They are happy I'm happy. It's awkward when meeting the first time, I know. But they like you, I can tell."

"You are better at gauging their reaction than I am. Are you sure your father will go along with it?"

She laughed. "Yes. He was worse with Tom. Of course we were still teenagers when we were first dating, but he even asked Tom for his five-year plan. Like a high school kid had such a thing. Relax, Zack. What's not to like?"

"As long as you keep thinking that way," he said, kissing her. "I'll go clean up and change and pick you and Danny up at six-thirty."

"See you then."

While Susan showered she considered the afternoon meeting. Her parents had been more concerned than she expected, but who could blame them. She'd agreed to marry a man she hardly knew, who had no family or even friends in the area.

Yet she knew it was going to be a happy marriage. Zack gave her security and contentment and yet excited her as no man had before. She was looking forward to finding a place together—as she and Tom had. Making a home for their family. Sharing holidays and birthdays. Watching Danny grow to manhood.

She also liked the idea of maybe adopting a child or two to complete their family. She knew Zack would want an older child—as he'd been when available for adoption. He'd never been chosen. Maybe they could change the life of a boy or girl and include them in their family.

The rest of the weekend passed quickly. The Molinas spent as much time with their grandson— and new son-in-law-to-be—as they could. Susan was pleased everyone seemed to get along, but there was no strong bond forged. It would take time. Her parents had known and loved Tom for years. It would take a while for Zack to find his way with them. She hoped they would make every effort. It was important to her that he found acceptance with her family. He'd been without one of his own all his life. She wanted him to be part of hers.

Monday morning her parents flew home. Susan went to work as normal. When she returned home that evening, Zack was home with Danny.

"Where's Edith?" she asked, after appropriate greetings had been exchanged.

"I sent her home about a half hour ago. I came by after my hours at the preschool. Brad also came this afternoon and Phillip Goldstein. We just about have the playground up to code."

"Let me change and I'll start supper."

"We can order in. I want to talk to you about looking for a house. It takes a bit of time after we find a place to close escrow. I'd like to move right in after we get married."

"Sounds fine to me. I'll be right back."

He had brought several sheets of listings in different towns on Long Island. After ordering in a Chinese dinner, they sat together and looked at the different properties. All were waterfront dwellings. Some were huge with matching price tags.

"We can't afford these," Susan said at last. The one in West Islip that was pictured on one leaflet was an ideal home. She'd love to see inside. But no use going there; it was way out of their price range.

"Yes, we can," he said, studying another.

She looked at him. "We can?" Just how much money did this future husband of hers have? The homes were in the millions of dollars.

He glanced at her, caught her gaze. "What?"

"Just how much can we afford?" she asked.

He shrugged. "I'll let you know if we go over budget. None of these will break the bank."

"You've saved more than a million dollars?" she asked in disbelief.

"I earn a lot of money, plus hardship bonuses. I've invested pretty well, and it just keeps growing."

She looked at Danny and then gazed around her apartment. "I can't believe this," she murmured.

"Hey, it's just money."

"You're rich."

"Well-off, I'd say."

"How well-off?"

"I don't know offhand. Do you want me to get my financial advisor to fax you a copy of my portfolio?" he asked whimsically.

"I don't even have a financial advisor. Zack, are you sure about getting married? I'm not bringing much to the union."

He put down the papers and reached for her hands. "You are bringing yourself and Danny, both beyond price. Never let money come between us."

Susan smiled at his reply. Tom had made a good living for them, but it looked as if Zack was in a class by himself. She vowed to do all she could to make sure he was as happy as she was with their marriage.

When the Chinese food arrived, Zack helped Danny wash his hands and soon they were all eating—Zack with chopsticks.

Danny watched, fascinated. "I want sticks," he said.

"You won't be able to eat with them," his mother said.

"Zack can. I can do it, too."

"It takes practice," Zack said. He took another set of chopsticks from the pile in the center of the table. Breaking them apart, he rubbed them together to make sure they were smooth for little boy hands.

"This is how you hold them," he said, patiently showing Danny the way.

Danny dropped everything he tried to pick up. He grew frustrated and before long threw the chopsticks across the room. "They're stupid," he said, his lower lip coming out.

"Go over and pick them up," Zack said.

Danny glared at him. "No."

"Danny," Susan began.

"Please, let me. If he doesn't recognize my authority in some things, it'll make for a bumpy road. Danny we do not throw things in this home. Please go and pick them up—now!" Zack said.

Danny stared at him for a moment longer then grudgingly got off his chair and went across the room to retrieve the chopsticks.

When he put them on the table and climbed back into his chair, Zack said, "Thank you. If something makes you frustrated, you need to find other ways to display that rather than throwing things. Can you remember that?"

Danny nodded, looking at his mother, his eyes filling with tears.

Susan wanted to grab him up and comfort him,

but she knew Zack was right and Danny needed to remember that.

"Eat your dinner with your fork. You can learn chopsticks when you're big like Zack."

"I don't like Zack," Danny said.

Susan saw Zack's expression go blank. She knew the childish words had hurt.

"Maybe not right this minute, but you'll like him again soon. Eat your dinner." To Zack, she said, "Kids say that all the time. The first time Danny said he h-a-t-e-d me I thought I'd never stop crying. It broke my heart. But he forgot he said it about ten minutes later. Kids say things they don't mean."

Zack nodded and resumed eating. Susan wished she could go comfort him. But he, like Danny, had lots to learn about making a family. There would always be some hiccups along the way.

Monday night set the stage for the rest of the week. Zack came to the apartment when he finished working at the school. He and Susan would have dinner together, sometimes preparing it themselves, sometimes ordering in. They spent time with Danny and once he was in bed each evening, would look at different real estate offerings, read about school districts and try to agree on the best place to live.

Thursday night when they sat together after Danny went to bed, Zack put his arm around Susan. "I have to fly to Washington in the morning. They moved up my physical."

"That's short notice."

"I said I'd take any cancellation. Once I'm cleared, I'll talk to the projects director and see what plans they have for any building projects in this area."

"And if not?"

"Then I quit and find something around here."

"That's risky."

"Hey, I'm good at what I do. I'll find a job, don't worry."

"When will you be home?"

"I'll stay in D.C. for the night, get an early flight back on Saturday. It's another workday at the school, and I think the last. Several different parents came during the week to work when I did, which helped move along faster than originally anticipated."

"Your being there is what moved it along faster," she said. "You've been wonderful."

He pulled her closer and kissed her.

Susan loved their quiet evenings together. They talked about everything, from current events, to books they both liked—she mysteries, he biographies. They discussed moving some favorite pieces of furniture with them and getting rid of the rest and buying new. And twice Zack brought up getting a puppy. Susan was not convinced.

"You'll call me after you see the doctor," Susan said when she walked him to the door later.

"Of course. As soon as I know. See you Saturday."

Susan closed the door softly and leaned against it. She would miss him until Saturday. She was getting spoiled with his constant presence. At least Danny had behaved better after his brief tantrum on Monday. She wanted Zack to love him as much as she did.

Susan, Betsy and other mothers were doing the last of the cleanup on Saturday when Zack strode into the room. He'd called Friday afternoon, but she'd missed the call because she had been in a meeting. Everything was fine, had been his message. She thought he might call last night, but he hadn't. She saw him as soon as he stepped in the room and met him halfway, almost running the last few steps. He caught her in his arms and kissed her.

The calls and clapping of the other mothers ended the kiss. Susan felt embarrassed, but the good-natured teasing had her smiling. Zack looked around dazed.

"He's been gone for sooo long," Betsy said. Then turned to the other mothers and added, "Since Thursday night at eleven."

Laughter followed her statement.

"I remember those days. Now I'd just as soon have the kit and caboodle gone for a weekend to have some me time," one of the mothers said.

"I'd like to stop working weekends," another added.

"We're out of here soon, and doesn't the school look great?" Betsy said.

"Last inspection on Monday. Mrs. Harper said Zack would be our point man," another added.

"Guess I better do a run-through to make sure everything is okay," he said, brushing his fingers against Susan's cheek. She smiled, wishing they could just go off and be alone this instant. Patience was a tough virtue to learn!

"So when's the wedding again?" Betsy asked as they went back to work.

"Last week in June. We're going to look at houses tomorrow," Susan said, polishing one window until not a streak or speck was left.

"We're going to miss you when you move," Betsy said.

"And Zack when other things around here need fixing," someone said.

"He might come back to help," Susan said, wondering if she would see these wonderful people again.

"He'll be needed at Danny's school when he starts kindergarten. You can't imagine all the activities that call for parents' help."

"Right now I can't imagine Danny in kindergarten. He's growing up too fast," Susan said.

"Amy is my fourth and will be starting in the fall. My oldest is already in sixth grade. The years fly by."

Susan had heard that from her own parents. She wished she could keep Danny little forever, but couldn't stop him growing. And she was finding such delight in seeing everything she took for granted being discovered by him. She could double her fun when Zack also got to be involved.

Zack left the school room with the laughter of the women still echoing in his ears. He hadn't cared about making a public display; he'd been anxious to see Susan. He had never expected to miss her so much in the short time they'd been apart. He'd had plenty to do. The physical had been grueling—to make sure he was capable of dealing with the hardships that arose with overseas work. Once he passed that, he'd gone to see the director of International Projects to let him know he was not going back.

When the man expressed dismay, Zack offered to see what they had in New York. Susan had strong ties to New York City and he didn't want to move her any farther away than Long Island. He had enjoyed his weeks in the city and would love the opportunity to discover all New York had to offer.

A new high-rise complex was in the planning stage and the director of Domestic Projects jumped at the chance of having a man of Zack's background and knowledge be a key player. Zack could start work in early June. Time enough for him to return to the job site in the Middle East and wind up his affairs there.

If he missed Susan this much after being gone only overnight, what would a week or longer in the Middle East be like?

He'd soon find out.

"Hey, how did it go?" Brad greeted him when Zack found him in the boiler room.

"I passed."

"So the next step?"

"Head back out to the job site to wind things up. Then I start a new assignment for the company here in New York."

"Man, that's great. I was worried you and Susan would be taking off for one of those far flung countries."

"I wouldn't take a family there. Beside, didn't you hear, we're looking for a house out on the Island."

"Almost as bad. Leaving here, I mean. It's been good working with you."

"Likewise, man."

Together Zack and Brad did an inventory of all the changes made. Zack double-checked that everything had been brought up to code and he had the documentation in order for the building inspector's visit on Monday. The school was in better shape than it had been in a long time.

"Want to go for a beer after this?" Brad asked.

"I heard that," Betsy said, coming into the hall. "What about us?" she asked as Susan stepped up beside her.

"Of course I meant for you two to be with us. How could we bear to be apart?" Brad said dramatically.

She cuffed him lightly on the shoulder. "Good answer. How about it, Susan, got time?"

"Up to Zack. I have a baby-sitter who's there for the entire day if I need her."

"And will be moving with them, when they go," Betsy added for her husband's sake. "We have the Jablonsky twins. And your niece when we need her."

"I know but they'll all graduate from high school before Bethany is old enough to watch herself. So who'll fill in then?"

Zack watched the interaction, enjoying the camaraderie. He'd had that at his work sites, but this was different. Couples with similar goals, working together. Usually when he had paid leave, he'd date the prettiest woman he could find—no strings attached. And certainly no feeling of belonging, of building something for the future together.

"Danny's okay. I checked before I came here," Zack said.

"Devoted daddy already," Betsy said. "Lucky you."

"I know. And not just for that," Susan said, joining Zack.

Several couples went out for a late lunch together. Zack enjoyed spending time with them— no dangers of mines, no endless sand with not a spot of shade to be had. He especially liked being linked to Susan. Everyone liked her and seemed to share in her happiness.

He was almost sorry the job at the school was over.

Not that there wasn't a lot to do in the next six weeks. Changes on every front.

On Sunday Zack rented a car and drove them all to look at houses. Susan sat in the front. A car seat was provided for Danny and he and Edith sat in the back. The older woman had protested she didn't need to go, but Zack had insisted. It was going to be her home as well, and he wanted her to have a vote.

"Well, I never," she said, smiling mistily at him. "Thank you, young man."

Susan grinned, and reached out to hug him. "You're so special," she whispered in his ear.

He'd do all he could to make her happy.

They drove slowly through the little towns to see what amenities they offered. Many had merely a supermarket and gas station. A couple had movie theaters and larger shopping areas. When they reached West Islip, he drove around, finding the schools and the churches from the map the real estate agent had sent him.

At last they met the agent and toured three houses. It was a long day. Danny ran around each one, not understanding the implication. Susan loved each kitchen and couldn't wait to try out some of her mother's recipes in them. Edith was enthusiastic about the in-law suites. One had a pool, which

Susan suspected would need to be constantly monitored lest a small child fall in.

On the drive back, Zack asked which she liked best.

"The second one, I think. Which did you like?"

"I liked that one. And the first."

"The first was way too big for our family."

"We may have more children," he reminded her.

"True."

"And I'd be around to help with housekeeping," Edith said from the back seat.

"Which did you like?" Susan asked.

"I liked them all. Each in-law unit is larger than the apartment I have now. And with a lovely garden to work in, how grand is that?"

"I don't know if I'd like gardening. Except for pots on the windowsill, I've never grown anything," Susan mused.

"Nothing much grows where I've been. All that green grass is amazing," Zack said.

"It looks like Central Park."

"We don't have to decide today. We have other listings we can check out," Zack said.

Zack was disappointed Susan hadn't fallen in love with one of the homes. He thought they all were nice. He had no idea how long it took to decide on a house. But he wanted her to pick the one they'd live in.

After dinner, Zack read to Danny. When his son fell asleep, Zack stayed beside him on the bed.

Danny had been excited about every house, running up the stairs, stamping his feet with no admonition to keep quiet not to bother the neighbors. He could see his son growing up in every one of them. Having friends over, playing in the pool if they had one. One day he'd be a teenager, and then off to college. Zack closed his eyes for a moment, appreciating all he might have missed out on had he not bumped into Susan that day. He couldn't imagine life now without her in it. Or Danny. He was eternally grateful.

When he rejoined Susan in the living room, she had an array of pamphlets spread out.

"I think I've found the one I like. We'd have to see it, but what do you think?"

She handed him one as he sat beside her. It described a brick colonial. The front lawn was beautiful, sloping gently to the road. He looked at the photographs of the rooms and backyard. There was a swing set already installed, a play area and covered sandbox. A pool was behind the house, surrounded by tall shade trees.

"We can go see it one day this week."

"Or next weekend," she said.

"I won't be here then," he said slowly.

"Where will you be?"

"I have to return to the job site and wind up my part. I'm leaving on Thursday and will be gone at least a week, maybe longer."

"Oh."

Disappointment was evident in her expression. Then worry replaced it.

"I'll be coming back," he said to reassure her.

"Unless you get blown up by another land mine," she said. "Can't you have someone else handle it?"

"It's my responsibility," Zack said.

She sighed. "It sounds so right when you tell Danny about responsibility, but I don't like this."

"Me, either, but I'll be home before you miss me."

"Not possible," she said, leaning against him in contentment.

They were silent for a few moments. Zack took a deep breath. They were growing closer day by day. But the largest obstacle to complete honesty lay before them. He wondered if she would tell him about Danny before they married. He wanted to reassure her why it didn't matter an iota. But so far nothing seemed to lend itself to that discussion.

He wanted all the old life cleared up—his work site in the Middle East, and the truth about Danny's paternity.

"Danny is a wonderful child. You've done a terrific job with him."

"Thanks. It hasn't always been easy. But I wouldn't trade him for anything."

Zack waited a moment. This was as perfect an opening as he could give her. He hoped she'd say something about it being hard to be a mother without the father, that when they had first adopted Danny she and Tom had planned a long life together.

But Susan remained silent.

Time was running out. He had to leave soon and he wanted her to know he knew about Danny and didn't care—in fact he relished the knowledge that she didn't have to raise him alone from now on. And that he was Danny's father.

It would be easier to tell her if she'd bring it up. But Susan continued to snuggle close, obviously content with her own thoughts. Or was she struggling to find a way to tell him? Was she the one who couldn't have children? It didn't have to have been Tom. Was she worried that would impact him someway? He wanted her whether she could have children or not. He didn't love her for her childbearing ability. He loved her for herself, and always would.

"The house you like has five bedrooms and an in-law unit."

"Mmm," she said.

"Could be we'd need to work to fill them up."

"Could be," she said.

"I'm not against adoption, you know," he said easily. "I wish someone had adopted me once my parents were no longer in the picture. But by then I was an older child—no one wanted to."

Now—she'd say how she couldn't bear for that to happen to another child, how they'd joyfully adopted Danny to give him a family and a permanent home.

"I'm sorry you weren't. You couldn't have been much older than Danny is now."

"But maybe not as charming. I can't imagine anyone seeing Danny and not wanting to adopt hm."

"Good thing he's not available," Susan said.

"Not now."

She sat up and looked at him, frowning slightly. "What do you mean? Nothing's going to happen to me."

"I didn't say it was."

"Then why say Danny's not available now?"

"I mean, not now. Earlier, maybe." How much of an opening did she need? His heart sank. Did she not trust him?

"Not ever. Even if something happens to me, my folks would make sure he was loved and taken care of."

"I could do that."

She smiled slightly and nodded.

"Danny's my son," he said.

"I'm so glad you think like that. I've heard stories about women marrying and the new husband didn't want anything to do with their children."

"I mean, he's really mine. I want to adopt him or change his last name, or something, so the world knows."

She pulled back a bit and tilted her head to better see him, obviously puzzled. "I think he should keep Tom's name. That's all the legacy

Tom left him. He would be your son in every way that counts."

"He is my son." Zack stood and walked to the window. "I had a detective find you, to tell me that he was all right, that he was being raised well. I didn't expect to actually meet you and Danny."

"What are you talking about?" Susan also rose and went to stand by him. "What detective?"

"The one I hired to find Danny. I didn't know his name, of course, just that Alesia had given up my baby for adoption."

Susan stared at him for a long moment. "Zack, Danny is Tom's son."

"I know you two adopted him. And that makes him just as much Tom's son as if Tom had fathered him. But you don't have to pretend with me. Together we can explain to Danny."

She stepped back, a look of horror on her face.

"Is that what all this has been about—Danny? You think he's yours? Is that why you insisted in getting to know me, getting to know Danny? You have a child somewhere and thought it was Danny?"

He turned to look at her. "I know it's Danny."

"Just what do you know?"

"Alesia gave up our son, he was adopted by T.J. and Susan Johnson of New York City. I came to New York when I was recuperating to see if I could get a glimpse of Danny. I wasn't planning to stop. But when you asked for my help, everything changed."

"Johnson is a very common name. What does T. J. stand for?"

"Thomas, I assume."

"It isn't me," she whispered. "It wasn't Tom. His middle name was Caldwell. I can prove it."

"What do you mean?" Zack asked, not understanding.

"Danny's my child. Mine and Tom's. I have pictures of me pregnant. Me in the hospital with Danny. Us at the christening. Tom and I did not adopt a child. Danny is our child. DNA can prove it in an instant." She stepped back, crossing her arms over her chest, watching him warily.

Zack stared at her in incomprehension. This was turning out all wrong. She was supposed to be relieved he knew the truth, not putting up barriers. "The detective said—"

"Well, I'd ask for my money back if I were you. He got it wrong." She turned her back on him, her hands rubbing her upper arms as if she were cold.

"All this is because you thought Danny's your son," she repeated.

"All what?" He stepped closer, aware he'd made a major blunder. It changed little. He still wanted Susan. It might take a little while to absorb the news she gave. Danny was not his son.

But he could still be Zack's. Once he and Susan were married. For a moment he took a breath. It would come out all right. He took a step closer.

"I'd like you to leave now, Zack," she said, her back still to him.

He took hold of her shoulders, turning her to face him. "I'm not leaving until we hash this out. I obviously made a mistake. So I'll keep looking for the boy Alesia and I had. It changes nothing for us."

"I think it changes everything. Please leave." She pulled away and went down the hall. He heard the bedroom door close.

Stunned, for a moment he couldn't move. *Danny wasn't his?* He loved that little boy. How could he have bonded so quickly with the child if there wasn't a connection?

The same way he had connected with Susan so quickly. He fell in love. For a moment Zack stared ahead without seeing anything. Love didn't recognize biology or blood. Love came from all directions, for all people.

He went down the hall and knocked on her door. "Susan, talk to me, please."

"No. Go away, Zack. Go away."

He waited a long moment. He should have waited to talk about this. There was a reason she never brought it up—there was nothing to bring up. "Susan, I can explain…"

There was no further sound from her room. Slowly he went to the door. He hesitated, then opened and stepped into the hall, closing the door behind him.

* * *

Susan heard the outer door close. She was leaning against her bedroom door, her heart breaking. She'd been so happy just moments before. Now the crushing pain was excruciating. She loved Zack. And he wanted to marry her because he thought Danny was his son. From the very beginning, he'd encouraged their relationship because of a mistaken idea her son was his. She could hardly breathe. Theirs was a relationship based on a lie. There would be no wedding, no new house on Long Island, no Zack in her life any more. She held her breath against the pain, but tears flowed and she crossed to curl up on her bed, sobbing as quietly as she could into her pillow.

After a while the tears ceased. Lying listlessly on the bed she tried to see where she might have realized that Zack hadn't been as in love as she would expect a man to be to get married. Granted, he'd never said he loved her, but she could excuse herself for seeing his every action construed that way. What other man would take on a woman and her child, plan dates that included activities for Danny, work at the preschool? Only, it wasn't for her. It was all for Danny. Or who he thought Danny was.

She had excused his lack of telling her he loved her due to his background. A child growing up without love might not know to say it. But now she realized that had little to do with his not telling her. He had been honest in that, at least.

It had been so hard to move on, to let herself trust

in the future again, to plan to build a new life. But she'd done it—only to have it slap her in the face. She would have done better to never have gotten involved than end up like this. She ached for Zack's arms to hold her. She yearned for his kisses. She would love to just sit beside him, and feel safe and cherished. She would miss planning for a future together. She would always miss *him*!

CHAPTER TEN

SUSAN woke to a splitting headache the next morning. She lay in bed feeling sad and lonely. Hearing Danny running down the hall, she tried to shake off her melancholia so not to upset her son. He would be unhappy enough when he finally realized Zack was out of their lives.

"Hi," he said, peeping around her door.

"Hi, yourself, little man. Come snuggle with me," she said.

He raced across the room and bound up into the bed. They snuggled together for a few minutes—all he could spare from his busy activities.

"I want to go to the park," he said, wiggling around.

"Okay, after we do some tidying of the house."

"'Kay." He struggled to get down. "Let's eat breakfast," he urged.

"I'll be right there. Don't climb up on the counter."

The last thing Susan wanted to do was move an inch. But she couldn't lie in bed the rest of her life. Today would be the first without Zack. She remembered when she'd had the first without Tom. The ache was just as piercing.

She'd have to tell Edith today that they wouldn't be moving. She knew the older woman had been happy with the expectation of change. Life would go along as it had. She'd stay in the poky apartment, fearing for Danny's safety as he grew older and began going outside by himself.

She'd pinch pennies to make ends meet. And sit in lonely silence in the evening hours once Danny was in bed.

Tears welled again. How could she stand it?

"Oh, Zack, why wasn't I enough?" she said softly, getting up to get dressed.

Once breakfast was finished, the apartment had been vacuumed and dusted and Danny dressed, Susan gathered their things for a trip to the park. She would not disrupt her son's routines. He asked for so little and she wished she could shower him with all things good.

The day was already warm and would probably be uncomfortably hot by midafternoon. But at this early hour it was comfortable and pleasant.

Susan held Danny's hand until they reached the park. He took off running to play with the children at the playground. She crossed the grass more slowly and sat on one end of a bench that held an older man who was watching the children. Probably a proud grandfather, she thought, smiling politely as she sat down. Her father loved to take Danny to the playground when her parents visited.

Time seemed to pass slowly as she mindlessly watched her son. If he needed her, she'd be there in an instant. Otherwise, she was content to let him interact with the other children. He'd look over occasionally and she'd wave. He played well with other children and from the shrieks of laughter, she knew they were all enjoying themselves.

Suddenly he got off the slide and began running across the grass. Susan jumped up. Was he chasing after someone who looked like Tom again? She passed the older gentleman and stopped, recognizing Zack heading toward her. Danny ran to him and Zack leaned over and picked him up, tossing him into the air. Susan could hear his laughter from where she stood.

Her heart began to pound. What was Zack doing here? Why had he come?

He settled Danny on one arm, talking to him as they walked steadily toward Susan. She wanted to run away and hide. Or stay and rail against him for letting her fall in love with him when he hadn't fallen in love with her. For raising her hopes and dreams only to have them smashed into dust.

When he drew closer, he put Danny on his feet and urged him back to the playground. His gaze caught hers and he walked purposefully toward her.

"Hi," he said.

She couldn't respond. She turned and went back to sit down, ignoring him completely. She was afraid to say anything lest tears began and never stopped.

Not deterred, Zack came and sat beside her. The older man glanced at them, then resumed watching the children.

"We need to talk," he said.

She shot him a look and shook her head. "I think we said all we needed to say last night."

"Not by a long shot," he said.

She shifted slightly, turning her shoulder to him. Maybe she should get Danny and return home.

He reached out and took her hand. When she tried to snatch it away, he held firmly.

"I want you to marry me. I want us to be a family. I want to raise Danny as my own."

"He's not yours."

"I didn't say he was, I said as my own."

"Go find your own son."

"Maybe. In time."

She looked at him, curious. "Why not now?"

"I have to get this straightened out first. Time enough later to see if that boy is happy and doing well. Which is what I started out doing here. I was only going to walk by the school, see Danny and then move on. Fate, angels, whatever changed that when you asked me for help. One thing led to another."

She looked away, thinking how she had fallen in

love with the man and he'd been there for a different reason.

"When Danny ran to greet me just a moment ago, love pure and simple shone from his eyes."

"He loves you."

"And you love me. Funny. All my life I wanted someone to love me, really love me. And when it happened, I didn't even see it."

Susan felt her eyes moisten with tears again. How sad to long for love. Every child should at least have that. Zack hadn't.

"Love grows best when it's returned," she mumbled, swallowing hard, trying to prevent the tears from spilling over.

"I walked all the way back to my hotel last night, stunned that you'd turned me out. It gave me a taste of what life would be like without you in it forever. I can't do it."

"Do what?"

"Face life without you. I'm not good at this, Susan, but I love you. The feelings I have for you are stronger than any I've ever had before. I may not be good at it, but I think these feelings will last a lifetime."

"You're just saying that. You managed fine all your life before finding me, you'll do fine the rest of your life without me," she said.

"But why should I? I love you. You love me. Let's get married. Build on the future together. Grow old together."

"Good idea," the older man said. "Love doesn't come to everyone more than once. By the child you have, I'm guessing this is your second chance, ma'am. I never got it. My wife died thirty years ago. My one daughter and now her children are all I have. I wish I'd met another woman I wanted to spend my life with."

Susan looked around Zack at the man.

"He only wanted me because he thought Danny was his son."

"Doesn't sound like it now," the man countered.

She blinked and looked at Zack. "Do you really love me?"

"Oh God, you don't know how much," he said, drawing her into his arms and kissing her soundly.

Danny called something from the playground, but Susan couldn't hear him. She only heard the beating of her heart as she returned Zack's kisses. From the depths of despair to the heights of joy in an instant. Was this real?

"So you'll marry me as planned?" Zack asked a moment later.

She hesitated only a second then nodded, feeling fearful and excited at the same time.

"Let me be the first to wish you both a long and happy life together," the older man said. He smiled at them, then rose and beckoned to two children. They ran to him, calling him Grandpa, and the trio walked away from the park.

"I do love you," Zack said, holding her close. "I'll do anything to make up for the heartache of last night."

"You don't need to do anything—not if you truly love me. That's all I wanted. But what about your quest for your child?"

"Maybe together we can find him and make sure he's okay. Families are formed by love, not only biology. If he's happy in his adoptive home, why would I want to wrest that from him? Maybe later we can approach them and let them know who we are and that we would always be available if he wants some kind of relationship. His parents may not wish that. Which, hard as it is to think about, would be okay. I would not rock his security for anything. Look at what happened to Danny when Tom died. I never want another child to go through something like that."

"Danny adores you. I was so scared for him when I thought you were out of our lives. Those hours last night were the worst I've had in years," Susan said.

"I never expected to find a woman like you. Never thought of myself as a married man. But now I can't wait. I'll be getting a wife and son all at once. And maybe we can add to our family when the time is right."

"Works for me. I always wanted several children. I'd love to have a baby with you."

"I would, too, but I would never love it more than Danny."

"No, the good thing about love is that it's infinite. You'll love our next child as much, and the one after that as well."

"How many are we going to have?" Zack asked.

"As many as we want and can afford. I would not mind adopting one or two, either, and having some of our own."

"Then the sky's the limit, my love." He kissed her.

EPILOGUE

Zack read the report from the detective. He slid it across the dining room table to Susan.

"Think he's got it right this time?" she asked, picking it up to read. Dinner had ended a little while ago. Danny was outside in the backyard playing with the puppy. Edith had gone to fuss in the garden while it was still daylight. Twilight came earlier each day in September.

"Maybe. This T.J. Johnson lives in Queens and works as an accountant. His wife's a librarian. They have a nice apartment and the child's name is Tommy, Junior. What do you think?" Zack asked, pointing to the photograph of a family at a company picnic somewhere.

"They look happy," she said, glancing up at her husband. "What do you think?"

"I hope they're as happy as we are. It's what I wanted, to know that he was well cared for and happy."

"Now what?"

"I think I'll ask Josh for his advice. Maybe have

him contact them just to see if they need anything, to let them know I'm here if they do." Josh was their new next door neighbor, fast becoming a friend. He was an attorney specializing in family law.

"Sounds like a plan. I'm happy with whatever you decide," Susan said. "If you want to go meet them, I'll go with you."

"If they want that. Or maybe just knowing we're in the background will make things easier for them."

Zack rose and came around the table, taking her hand and helping her up. "I'll help with the dishes if you want," he said, leaning over to kiss her.

"He's not your only child, you know," she said smiling up at him.

"No, Danny's mine in every way that counts."

"And he's not your only one, either," Susan said. "We're pregnant. I think it happened on our honeymoon."

Zack stared at the woman he loved in disbelief. "We're going to have a baby?"

She nodded, her happiness shining from her eyes. "And I got brochures from the adoption agency in town. Honey, if you want, we could have a house full before much longer."

Zack hugged her, lifting her off her feet and twirling around. Susan laughed and reached up to kiss him when he set her back on the ground.

"I love you, Zack," she said.

"I love you, sweetheart, now and forever." He sealed his vow with a kiss. In his quest for his son, he'd found the only woman he had ever loved. And she'd given him the family he'd never had. Amazing.

* * * * *

*In honor of our 60th anniversary,
Harlequin® American Romance® is celebrating
by featuring an all-American male each month,
all year long with*
MEN MADE IN AMERICA!
*This June, we'll be featuring American men
living in the West.*

Here's a sneak preview of
THE CHIEF RANGER by Rebecca Winters.

*Chief Ranger Vance Rossiter has to confront the
sister of a man who died while under Vance's
watch…and also confront his attraction to her.*

"Chief Ranger Rossiter?" The sight of the woman who'd stepped inside Vance's office brought him to his feet. "I'm Rachel Darrow. Your secretary said I should come right in."

"Please," he said, walking around his desk to shake her hand. At a glance he estimated she was in her midtwenties. Her feminine curves did wonders for the pale blue T-shirt and jeans she was wearing. "Ranger Jarvis informed me there's a young boy with you."

The unfriendly expression in her beautiful green eyes caught him off guard. "Yes," was her clipped reply. "When we arrived in Yosemite the ranger told me I couldn't go anywhere in the park until I talked to you first."

"That's right."

"Knowing you wanted this meeting to be private, he offered to show my nephew around Headquarters."

So this woman was the victim's sister…. "What's his name?"

"Nicky."

The boy who haunted Vance's dreams now had a name. "How old is he?"

"He turned six three weeks ago. Were you the man in charge when my brother and sister-in-law were killed?"

"Yes. To tell you I'm sorry for what happened couldn't begin to convey my feelings."

The woman's gaze didn't flicker. "I won't even try to describe mine. Just tell me one thing. Was their accident preventable?"

"Yes," he answered without hesitation.

"In other words, the people working under you fell asleep on your watch and two lives were snuffed out as a result."

Hearing it put like that, he had to set the record straight. "My staff had nothing to do with it. I, myself, could have prevented the loss of life."

Ms. Darrow's expression hardened. "So you admit culpability."

"Yes. I take full blame."

A look of pain crossed over her features. "You can just stand there and admit it?" Her cry echoed that of his own tortured soul.

"Yes." He sucked in his breath.

"I work for a cruise line. Aboard ship, it's the captain's responsibility to maintain rigid safety regulations. If a disaster like that had happened while he was in charge he would have been relieved of his command and never given another ship again."

Rachel Darrow couldn't know she was preaching to the converted. "If you've come to the park with the intention of bringing a lawsuit against me for negligence, maybe you should." It would only be what he deserved.

"Maybe I will."

In the next instant, she wheeled around and hurried out of his office. Vance could have gone after her, but it would cause a scene, something he was loath to do for a variety of reasons. In the first place, he needed to cool down before he approached her again.

The discovery of the Darrows' frozen bodies had affected every ranger in the park. A little boy had been orphaned—a boy whose aunt was all he had left.

* * * * *

*Will Rachel allow Vance to explain—
and will she let him into her heart?
Find out in*
THE CHIEF RANGER
*Available June 2009
from Harlequin® American Romance®.*

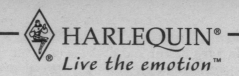

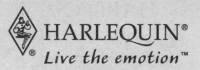

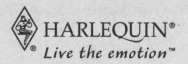

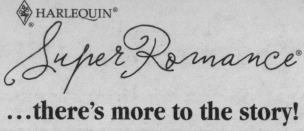
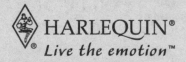